THE DUKE AND THE PREACHER'S DAUGHTER

Benedicta gave a little cry and threw herself against the Duke.

"I am so frightened I may . . . disappoint you."

He pulled her closer to him.

"Do you think I want you to know anything but what I shall teach you?" he asked. "I adore your ignorance, your purity."

He spoke with a fervor she had never heard before.

"I was the first man who had ever kissed you. I shall also be the only man, and the last."

Benedicta gazed at him in awe.

"How could there be anyone else but you?" she asked wonderingly.

Very tenderly the Duke looked down into her eyes.

"You are mine," he said.

He kissed her until he could feel her soft and pliant against him, until his lips had awakened in her the first flickering flames of desire . . .

Bantam Books by Barbara Cartland
Ask your bookseller for the books you have missed

Barbara Cartland's Library of Love series

Barbara Cartland's Ancient Wisdom series

Barbara Cartland

The Duke and the Preacher's Daughter

BANTAM BOOKS
TORONTO · NEW YORK · LONDON

THE DUKE AND THE PREACHER'S DAUGHTER
A Bantam Book / January 1979

ISBN 0–553–12841–8

Published simultaneously in the United States and Canada

Bantam Books are published by Bantam Books, Inc. Its trade-
mark, consisting of the words "Bantam Books" and the por-
trayal of a bantam, is Registered in U.S. Patent and Trademark
Office and in other countries. Marca Registrada. Bantam
Books, Inc., 666 Fifth Avenue, New York, New York 10019.

PRINTED IN THE UNITED STATES OF AMERICA

Author's Note

Private duelling was never as prevalent in England as in France, although under James I it became, in the words of Sir Francis Bacon, an "unbridled evil."

In George III's reign, 172 duels were reported in which 91 persons were killed. In 1809 a notable duel took place between Viscount Castlereagh, the Secretary for War, and George Canning, the Foreign Secretary.

Up to 1840 the British Military Code authorised duelling, but it became a Military Offence in the Army Act of 1881. Thereafter, duels took place abroad—usually at Calais or Boulogne.

Chapter One

1817

Footmen with powdered wigs and gold-braided livery extinguished the candles round the big Dining-Room, leaving alight only those in the golden candelabrum on the dining-table.

The six candles created an oasis of light which was reflected not only on the magnificent ornaments but on the table itself.

This, in the fashion set by the Prince Regent, had no cloth, but was polished to reflect like a mirror everything upon it.

The Butler put on the table a decanter of port and one of brandy, standing in their ornate coasters, and after a glance round the room he withdrew, followed by the footmen.

The Duke of Kingswood leant back in his chair and said to the gentleman sitting beside him:

"You have been strangely quiet this evening, Bevil. Is there something on your mind?"

The gentleman he addressed hesitated a moment before he replied:

"You know me so well, Nolan, that I might have guessed you would suspect that I have something to tell you."

The Duke waited with a cynical expression on

his face. It would have proclaimed to anybody watching him that he was quite sure that nothing he was told would surprise him and it would be doubtful if it even would interest him.

It was strange that a man who had such vast possessions and could in fact command anything he desired should look so blasé and so bored with life.

It was not only his friends, and he had a great number, but also the lovely ladies who tried to capture and hold him in their toils who had found it almost impossible to keep the Duke's attention for long.

His companion was very different.

Major Bevil Haverington was in fact the same age as the Duke but he looked younger, which was due perhaps to his enjoyment of the life he lived and also to his simple, uncomplex nature, which ensured that he was pleased with almost everything.

In a way it was strange that the two men should be such close friends, but they had gone to Eton and Oxford together, then had served in the same Regiment through the long, gruelling years in the Peninsula.

It had been a campaign which could have made any man age quickly, and perhaps, as in the Duke's case, look at life thereafter with prejudiced eyes.

Major Haverington had in fact enjoyed every battle, and as a regular soldier he had no intention of giving up his Regiment now that there was peace.

The Duke, on the other hand, although he had been one of the youngest Commanders on the battlefield, had been forced on his father's death to buy himself out.

He had returned home to administer his estates and take his place not only in the House of Lords but in the County and at Court.

The Prince Regent had in fact welcomed his home-coming with open arms, and so had a great number of other people in the *Beau Monde,* mainly for some selfish reason of their own.

It was unusual for the Duke to be alone with

only one friend at Kingswood, but after receiving unexpectedly a letter from his Agent, he had decided that his presence there was necessary and had invited Bevil Haverington to drive down with him from London.

Major Haverington had been only too glad to oblige.

He preferred being alone with his friend, when they could talk over the battles they had fought side by side and reminisce in a way which they knew the majority of their friends found extremely boring.

Ever since they had arrived in the magnificent house which had belonged to the Wood family since the time of Charles II, the Duke had sensed a reserve and a feeling of unrest about the Major, which was unlike him.

Now he knew he was about to hear the explanation, and he was quite certain that if it concerned himself it would be, if not unpleasant, certainly nothing that would add to his enjoyment of the evening.

He took a sip of port before he said:

"Come on, Bevil, out with it! If there is one thing I dislike, it is to anticipate the worst!"

"It is not as bad as that," Major Haverington replied. "At the same time, you will not be pleased."

"That will be nothing new," the Duke said sardonically.

"It concerns Richard."

"I might have guessed that!"

"He is making a fool of himself."

"That is certainly nothing unusual."

"This time it is rather more serious. He has asked Delyth Maulden to marry him and she has accepted!"

It was obvious from the way he stiffened that the Duke was surprised, and his eyes were hard as he exclaimed:

"I always knew Richard was a fool, but not such a damned fool as to marry Delyth Maulden!"

"He is too good a catch for her to let him go," the Major said simply.

He fiddled with the stem of his glass as he went on:

"You know, ever since Gosport refused to marry her she has been trying to find somebody of importance to take his place."

"Gosport's mother managed to save him at the very last moment," the Duke said. "She had almost got him to the Church door."

There was silence as both men were thinking of the weak, good-humoured young Marquis of Gosport, who had cast himself and his title at the feet of the most acclaimed and certainly the most cunning beauty in London.

He had nearly been saddled with her for the rest of his life.

Lady Delyth Maulden, daughter of the dissolute and impoverished Duke of Hull, had burst upon the Social World five years earlier.

There was no doubt that she was exceedingly beautiful, and the Bucks and Beaux of St. James's, always ready to be captivated by a fresh and lovely face, had declared her an "Incomparable" and drunk her health in even deeper draughts than were usual.

It was, of course, the great hostesses who had first discovered that Lady Delyth was as dissolute as her father, with morals which even in an immoral age could not be accepted without protest.

She took lover after lover, and although she might have attempted to keep her *amours* discreet, regular wagers were soon laid at White's Club as to who would be the next victim.

The Duke had heard that his young cousin and heir presumptive, Richard Wood, was infatuated, but he had in fact paid little attention to the gossip.

It would do the boy no harm, he had thought, to learn the hard way that Delyth would extract from his pocket every penny he possessed and a great deal he did not.

If he was disillusioned in the process, it would doubtless make him more particular next time as to where he cast his heart.

But that Delyth would plan to marry the boy had never entered his mind, and now he realised that he had been almost as foolish as his heir.

Delyth Maulden would of course consider Richard a good catch, seeing that it was known by everybody that the Duke had said not once but a dozen times that he had no intention of marrying.

It had been such a sensational statement from a man of such high rank that it was impossible for people not to be curious as to why he intended to stay a bachelor when, according to all the rules and traditions of the nobility, he should be anxious to have a son.

The Duke did nothing to assuage their curiosity.

He merely said that he had no wish to take a wife and that when he was dead, which would not be for a great many years, Richard would undoubtedly take his place most admirably.

Nobody could quite believe that he would remain resolute in such a contention.

Yet, four years had elapsed since he had inherited the title, and his love-affairs—and there were a great number of them—were always conducted with lovely, sophisticated women who invariably had husbands.

The Duke, however, had a great pride of family.

He had not expected when he was young ever to inherit the title, as his father had been a second son, while his uncle had a son and heir and every prospect of being able to add to his family as the years passed.

However, by several strange quirks of fate, accidents, and illness, the Duke had been swept into the seat of power when he least expected it.

Although his private life, which he considered his own, was slightly reprehensible, his public appearance upheld all the dignity and consequence of his position.

He fulfilled his duties punctiliously and with a formality which at times could be quite awe-inspiring.

Therefore, the idea that somebody like Lady

Delyth Maulden should become the Duchess of Kingswood and Chatelaine of the Mansion in which they
were now sitting was more of a shock than even his
friend Bevil Haverington had envisaged.

"Dammit all!" he said aloud. "Why marriage?"

"Delyth has seen to that. As I told you, Richard
is infatuated to the point where he would try to give
her the moon and the stars, should she ask for them."

The Duke's lips tightened.

"When did you hear this?"

"I was told it last night, and thought I had better
keep the information from you until we could discuss
it quietly and alone."

"What is there to discuss?" the Duke asked
savagely. "Delyth Maulden has extracted a promise
of marriage from Richard, and she will not let him
go back on his word."

"I am afraid not," Major Haverington agreed.

The Duke sat almost like a statue and his friend
knew what he was thinking.

He had seen the same expression on his face
when they were facing the enemy, outnumbered and
strategically in an impossible position.

And yet, dozens of times in such circumstances
he had seen the Duke lead his troops out of what
seemed the certainty of annihilation and carry them
to victory almost by the force of his own will-power.

At the same time, the Major thought despairingly, war was one thing, love was another, and young
Richard was in it up to his neck.

As the Duke did not speak, the Major volun-
teered after a moment or two:

"As a matter of fact, they are not far from here
at the moment. They are staying at Tring Castle."

"Tring was a good soldier," the Duke said auto-
matically.

"He has been pretty wild since the war ended,"
Major Haverington added. "I found that one of the
parties I attended at the Castle was far too noisy
for my liking. But that is the sort of thing which Delyth
enjoys."

The Duke had a sudden vision of the same sort of parties which the Major was describing, taking place at Kingswood.

The idea made him wince.

He knew that when men and women were riotously drunk, treasures easily were damaged in the process, and they were far more difficult to replace than damaged reputations.

Clenching his fist, he brought it down heavily on the table, making the crystal glasses jump.

"I will not have it! Do you hear me, Bevil? I will not permit Richard to marry this woman."

"But how can you stop him?" the Major asked bluntly.

"Give me an idea. You used to be full of them when we were fighting in Portugal."

"If we were there," Major Haverington replied, "we could doubtless have Delyth kidnapped or send Richard home in a slow ship! But Portugal is one thing, England another."

There was a scowl between the Duke's eyes as he said:

"There must be something we can do. You know she ruined young Morpeth and he had to retire to the country."

"Without a penny to his name," Major Haverington agreed. "And Morpeth was not the only one. But where Richard is concerned she intends to be his wife, and although one may dislike her, you have to admit that she will grace the Kingswood diamonds."

"Not if I chuck every one of them into the lake with my own hands!" the Duke said violently.

His glass was empty and he reached for the decanter of port, then changed his mind and picked up the one containing brandy.

"If anything could make me feel uncivilised and ready to commit murder," he said, "it is the idea of Delyth Maulden making a fool of Richard, and of— me."

"There is one quite simple solution."

"What is that?"

"That you should get married and have an heir!"

As Major Haverington spoke, he saw a flash of anger in his friend's face that was frightening, even though he knew the Duke so well.

There was silence, then the Duke said quietly:

"Not even to save Richard or prevent Kingswood from being turned into a glorified brothel would I take a wife!"

"But why? Why have you got this ridiculous attitude with regard to matrimony?" Major Haverington asked.

As he spoke he thought that "ridiculous" was a mild way of expressing it.

Not only was the Duke one of the wealthiest men in England and his possessions were unequalled by any other nobleman, but he was in fact so attractive and so handsome that the women who pursued him were not activated only by his rank or by what he possessed.

The great majority loved him for himself.

Looking at the Duke, the Major could hear one woman saying brokenly:

"I loved Nolan. I loved him with all my heart. When he left me I knew it would be impossible for me ever to be happy again."

"Why should he leave you?"

"I wish I knew." She sighed. "There is something hard and reserved within him which no woman can touch; a block of ice which nobody can melt."

It was an extraordinary idea, the Major thought, but the same story had been repeated to him so many times that he had begun to believe it.

He knew from his own observation that while the Duke was prepared to accept the favours that beautiful women would offer him, he gave them in return nothing of himself.

He was generous, almost overwhelmingly so, but those who loved him were not content with diamonds and pearls, but desired his heart.

But they never had a chance of possessing it.

As if the Duke had no more to say on the subject,

he rose from the Dining-Room table, although he had not touched the glass of brandy.

The Major followed him and they walked along the wide corridors hung with magnificent pictures towards the great Library, where the Duke usually sat when he was alone or with a few men-friends.

The big, comfortable arm-chairs, the background of books that were the envy of scholars, the painted ceiling, and the gold-balustraded balcony running along the top of the walls were a delight to the eye.

The Major had always thought it was one of the most attractive rooms he had ever seen and particularly suitable as a background for its owner.

The Duke sat down in an arm-chair in front of the stone mantelpiece which craftsmen had brought to England from Italy early in the last century.

Although it was May, the nights were inclined to be chilly and there was a fire burning in the grate.

The Major stood in front of it.

"You know, Nolan," he said after a moment, "I am now regretting that I am the bearer of bad news. Perhaps it would have been best for you to have found out what was happening for yourself."

"I would rather I heard it from you than from anybody else," the Duke replied.

"That is what I hoped you would say," the Major remarked simply.

"At least you and I can be frank with each other," the Duke said. "And we know that if Richard marries Delyth Maulden he will soon discover that his life is a hell on earth."

"Because he loves her."

"That is what I am saying. Richard is trusting and idealistic."

The Duke paused, then his lips twisted cynically as he went on:

"Something which I ceased to be long before I was his age."

"What happened?"

"That I do not intend to tell you or anyone else,"

the Duke replied. "But it was sufficient for me to understand what he will go through."

"Then what can you do to prevent it?" the Major asked.

"There must be something," the Duke muttered.

They both were still saying more or less the same thing three hours later.

It was impossible for any other subject to hold their attention, and although both men tried, inevitably their thoughts returned to Delyth Maulden and her latest capture.

She had actually tried her wiles on both the Duke and the Major.

The Duke had been immune to every enticement she offered him, even the provocative invitation in her huge eyes and on her red lips.

Major Haverington had not received the full blast of Lady Delyth Maulden's allure, for the simple reason that he was not important or rich enough.

She had merely dallied with him at a party at Tring Castle, the one which he had spoken about to the Duke.

He could remember how lovely she had looked in the moonlight when she had insisted that he take her out onto the terrace.

She had looked at him from under her eye-lashes, and as they had leant over the balustrade she had moved a little nearer, and he had been conscious of the seductive scent of her hair and the low décolletage of her evening-gown.

He had nearly succumbed and behaved as she expected, but a burst of drunken laughter from the room behind them had saved him.

Firmly he had taken her back to join her raucous friends, and he had known that she was furious, and in fact after that she had considered him an implacable enemy.

The clock on the mantelpiece struck the hour and the Major looked up and exclaimed:

"It is one o'clock, and if we are going to ride at

the particularly early hour you usually favour in the morning, I am going to bed!"

"A wise decision," the Duke remarked. "We have expended a great many words tonight and are no further towards solving the problem than we were when we started."

"Perhaps I shall dream of a solution," the Major said, "but I think it is unlikely."

He walked towards the door, and when the Duke made no attempt to follow him he asked:

"Are you staying up?"

"For a little while," the Duke replied. "When I was in the Army I got into the habit of sleeping only for a few hours, and now I find it hard to break."

The Major yawned.

"Well, personally I am tired. Good-night, Nolan."

"Good-night, Bevil."

The door shut behind him and the Duke picked up a newspaper from the stool in front of the fire.

He opened *The Times*, but then laid it down on his knee and sat thinking.

What could he say? How could he persuade Richard that he was making the greatest mistake of his life?

He thought of the boy as an untrained recruit under his command, and he felt the protective urge towards him that he had felt for so many of the young men who had come out from England.

They had been forced to face the withering fire of the enemy and the discomforts of a campaign in which one night they would be billeted in some flea-infested hovel in a Portuguese village, and the next they would be bivouacking on a barren hillside without even a shrub or a tree to protect them from the elements.

He had known, however, that it was not only an unknown enemy or the idea of death that had frightened them, but that they might disgrace themselves in the eyes of their comrades.

He remembered moving amongst them, talking to them, sustaining them, encouraging them.

But a raw recruit had to obey his orders, and Richard was a free man.

The Duke looked round the Library and thought not only how beautiful it was but how peaceful.

How could he tolerate the people with whom Delyth Maulden associated turning the place into a bear-garden, as he had seen happen in other large houses?

The rowdiness of the young Bucks, which had been growing steadily since the beginning of the century, had been censured by the more sober-minded members of Society.

But it was difficult for them to say much when the behaviour they so deprecated had been encouraged by the Prince of Wales before he became Regent.

Now that he was older he had become more circumspect, although his long list of elderly mistresses was virulently deprecated by the cartoonists.

A way of social life once started was difficult to control, and some of the behaviour amongst the younger men had made the Duke wish that he had them under his command and could treat them with the severity they deserved.

Delyth Maulden headed a variety of attractive women who had laid aside their very femininity to take part in wild parties, crazy escapades, and indiscretions which in the past had been the hall-mark of actresses and prostitutes.

The future Duchess of Kingswood!

Delyth Maulden knew only too well that marriage to Richard meant that a great many doors which were closed to her now would be opened and she would have to be accepted in circles which previously had given her the "cold shoulder."

"The Duchess of Kingswood!"

The Duke said the words through gritted teeth, then turned his head in surprise as the door opened.

A footman stood waiting for his master's attention.

"What is it?" the Duke asked.

"Lord Tring has called to see you, Your Grace."

"At this hour of the night?" the Duke exclaimed. Then he added: "Show His Lorship in."

A few seconds elapsed while his visitor was being brought along the corridor, then the footman announced:

"Lord Tring—Your Grace!"

The Duke had only to glance at his visitor to realise that something was seriously amiss.

Lord Tring was still wearing his evening-clothes but he had pulled a pair of riding-boots over his skin-tight trousers which fastened under the instep, and his intricately tied cravat was slightly crumpled.

His hair, which had obviously been arranged in the wind-swept fashion introduced by the Prince Regent, was now merely untidy and flopping about his forehead.

"Good-evening, Tring," the Duke said in quiet, unhurried tones. "What brings you here at this time of night?"

The young man looked over his shoulder, waiting for the footman to close the door. Then he said in a voice that was curiously unsteady:

"I had to come, Sir! You are the only person who I felt would know what to do and be able to cope."

He spoke, the Duke knew, as a young soldier addressing his Commanding-Officer, and there was an expression of trust in his eyes which was almost movingly familiar.

"Have a drink," the Duke suggested, "and tell me what has happened."

As if he felt in urgent need of it, Lord Tring went to the grog-tray on the table in the corner of the room, which the Duke had indicated.

He poured himself out a large brandy and drank it down in one gulp. Then he pushed back his hair from his forehead with a hand that trembled, and came back towards the Duke.

"It is—Richard, Sir!"

"Richard?" the Duke exclaimed. "What has happened to him?"

He saw Lord Tring take a deep breath, then he replied:

"He shot Sir Joceline Gadsby, then tried to kill himself!"

The Duke remained quite calm. His eyes searched Lord Tring's face as if he sought to substantiate the words he had just heard.

Some seconds passed before he said, again calmly:

"Sit down! You look as if you have ridden hard."

"When I saw what had happened," Lord Tring replied, sinking down into a chair as if his legs would no longer carry him, "I knew that the only person who could help would be you."

"Why did Richard shoot Gadsby?" the Duke asked.

He remembered the Baronet as a rather fulsome, over-talkative member of White's Club, whom he had gone out of his way to avoid.

He thought the man was an outsider and wondered how he had ever been admitted as a Member.

Then, as he thought of it, he knew what Lord Tring would reply.

"Richard—found him," His Lordship said in an embarrassed tone, "with—Lady Delyth."

"Where?"

"In—in bed, Sir!"

The Duke, who had been standing, sat down in an arm-chair as if he too needed its support.

"Tell me from the beginning!" he commanded.

"Richard arrived two days ago to stay with me," Lord Tring said, "and that night at dinner he announced that he and Lady Delyth were engaged to be married. Of course we toasted them and wished them every happiness."

"Of course!" the Duke commented sarcastically.

"Quite a number of the men in the house-party protested that they were broken-hearted, and half-jokingly tried to persuade Lady Delyth to change her mind."

The Duke thought she was unlikely to do that, and Lord Tring went on:

"I gathered that Sir Joceline was—an old friend, and therefore somewhat piqued that she was engaged."

The Duke knew that by saying "an old friend" Lord Tring meant in fact that Sir Joceline had been, like so many other men, Delyth Maulden's lover.

He was the type of man, he was sure, who would not take no for an answer even if she was engaged to somebody else.

"What happened tonight?" he asked.

"We went to bed early because most of us were going racing tomorrow morning. I was the last to go upstairs, and had not yet undressed because I was discussing with my valet what I should wear tomorrow.

"It was then, as we were talking, that I heard a sudden explosion. For a moment I thought I must be mistaken; then, as I thought it had come from a room on the first floor, not far from my own, it was followed by another.

"I pulled open the door, ran down the passage, and saw that the door of Lady Delyth's bed-room was open. . . ."

Lord Tring's voice died away as if he found it hard to go on.

"Tell me what you saw," the Duke prompted.

"Richard had obviously been standing at the foot of the bed, while Lady Delyth and Gadsby had been—together," Lord Tring said in a low voice. "Gadsby was dead, and there was blood all over the sheets."

"And Richard?" the Duke enquired.

"He was lying on the floor, with a bullet-wound over his heart!"

Lord Tring gave a little gulp as if it made him

feel sick to remember what he had seen, and the
Duke asked:

"What did you do then?"

"I went first to Richard, and realised that while
he was bleeding from a wound in his chest, he was
still alive. I have seen enough wounded men, Sir,
as you know, not to be mistaken."

"Yes, I know," the Duke said. "Go on!"

"I fetched my valet to help me and we picked
him up and carried him to his own room, which was
not far way. Then I went back to the bed-room."

"What was Lady Delyth doing when you returned?"

"She had got out of bed and put on something
to cover her," Lord Tring replied. "She was pale but
quite composed.

" 'Joceline is dead,' she said to me, 'and unless
you can think of some way out of this mess, Richard
will hang for it.'

" 'Do not speak to anybody, and keep your door
closed,' I said to her. Then, Sir, I came to you."

Again Lord Tring looked at the Duke with the
eyes of a man who thinks with utter relief that he
can cast his burden upon somebody else.

The Duke rose to his feet.

"Quite right," he said. "You can trust your valet
to look after Richard in your absence?"

"He was with me in the Regiment, Sir, and he
knows more about wounds and how to treat them
than half the Doctors we had with us."

'That would not be difficult,' the Duke thought
to himself, but aloud he said:

"I will order a horse and ride back with you. It
will only take me a few minutes to change my
clothes. Pour yourself another drink."

He walked across the Hall, ordered his horse
from a footman on duty, then walked quickly but
with dignity up the Grand Staircase.

His valet was waiting for him in his bed-room.

"I am going over to Tring Castle to fetch Mr.
Richard, Hawkins," the Duke said. "He has had an

accident and will require careful nursing. I shall put him in your hands."

"What has happened, Your Grace?" the valet enquired.

"Mr. Richard has been wounded," the Duke said cautiously.

"In a duel, Your Grace?"

"Yes, Hawkins, that is right—in a duel," the Duke replied.

The horse the Duke had ordered had been brought to the door only a few seconds before His Grace descended the stairs.

Lord Tring was waiting for him in the Hall.

He still looked pale and somewhat stricken but he had tidied his hair and adjusted his cravat, and the Duke knew as he joined him that he instinctively straightened himself as if he were going into action.

"Will we bring Richard back in one of your carriages or mine?" the Duke asked.

"Mine are at your service, Sir."

"Very well. Order one as soon as we arrive," the Duke replied.

They rode down the oak-bordered drive and out through the great gold-tipped iron gates, with their lodges on either side.

Crossing the main highway, they took to the fields and rode as the crow flies, cross-country towards Tring Castle.

They moved so quickly that conversation between them was impossible.

As both men were good riders and were mounted on superlative horse-flesh, nothing was to be heard but the thunder of hoofs, and the miles between the two great houses were quickly covered.

The moonlight made the way easy and illuminated the ancient Castle to which every succeeding generation had added, making it appear very romantic.

Now it concealed, the Duke thought, something sordid and degrading, a scandal which had to be hidden at all costs.

Barbara Cartland

A duel was accepted as an honourable way of settling a quarrel, but the murder of a married man was punishable by death.

He had no intention, if it was humanly possible, of letting Richard suffer for a crime which he knew was entirely the fault of the woman who had not been faithful to him, even on the first night of their engagement.

When they reached the front of the Castle, Lord Tring flung himself off his horse, while the Duke descended leisurely as if he was in no great hurry.

There were two night-footmen on duty in the Hall, who hurried forward to take their hats and riding-gloves.

Lord Tring paused as if waiting for the Duke to tell him how to proceed.

"Will you order a carriage?" the Duke reminded him.

"Oh, yes, of course!" Lord Tring said.

He gave the order and one of the flunkeys hurried off towards the stables. Then the Duke mounted the stairs and Lord Tring led him along a wide corridor off which opened the State-Rooms.

It struck the Duke as exceedingly distasteful that Lady Delyth had been allotted the room which had been occupied by Lord Tring's mother until her death.

It was one of the sights of the Castle, and it was reputed that Queen Elizabeth had slept there on one of her journeys round the countryside, when the size of her retinue and the expensive celebrations to honour her presence practically bankrupted her hosts.

Lord Tring knocked, then without waiting for a reply entered the room.

Delyth Maulden, wearing an extremely attractive negligée, was sitting at the dressing-table in front of the mirror.

Her long dark hair was streaming over her shoulders, and the face she turned as the two gentlemen entered was quite composed and, as the Duke had to admit savagely, exceedingly attractive.

On the bed lay Sir Joceline, dead from a bullet which had hit him accurately in the heart.

Ignoring Lady Delyth, the Duke walked to the bed and looked down at the dead man.

"Have him dressed," he said to Lord Tring. "Move him into the corridor, then change and destroy the sheets. Your valet can do that without anyone else in the house knowing anything about it."

The Duke turned towards the door.

"I would now like to see Richard."

"Yes, of course," Lord Tring replied.

"Have you nothing to say to me?" Lady Delyth interposed.

The Duke stood still. Then he answered:

"You will say that a duel took place in the corridor between two men who had imbibed too freely at dinner."

He paused before he continued:

"You were fully dressed when it happened. It was a quarrel which began as you walked up the stairs together, over some triviality—such as who should escort you out riding tomorrow."

The Duke looked at her and added:

"Let me make this clear: I am not inventing this charade to save your reputation, but wholly to prevent Richard from being arrested for murder."

"He is an hysterical fool!" Lady Delyth exclaimed contemptuously.

"I agree with you," the Duke replied, "and a blind and stupid one, or he would have known you for what you are—a harlot!"

His voice was like a whip. Then he turned away and, followed by Lord Tring, left the room.

When they entered the room to which Richard had been carried, the Duke saw that his cousin was lying on the bed, still dressed, except that his shirt was open down the front and his chest had been bandaged by the valet.

He looked very pale, but when the Duke put his hand on his forehead the skin felt warm, and when he felt his pulse it was beating, although faintly.

"I will take him home," the Duke said to Lord Tring, "and when I have left and Sir Joceline's body has been dressed, ride over to the High Sheriff. He was a friend of your father's and I know he will do his best to help you."

"I will do what you say," Lord Tring replied. "And thank you, Sir."

There was no mistaking the gratitude in his voice, and the Duke knew that he felt that his Commanding-Officer had solved his problem just as he had solved so many others in the past.

"When I have gone," the Duke said, "make quite sure that you and that woman tell the same story about what occurred. It does not matter much what you say, as neither of the contestants will be in a position to contradict you."

His voice was harsh, because he knew that Richard was seriously hurt and might even be dying from his self-inflicted wound.

At the same time, although it was perhaps dangerous to move him, the Duke knew that he would rather trust him to Hawkins's nursing than to anyone else's.

Like Harris, Hawkins had fought beside his master, but Lord Tring was younger and Hawkins had been with the Duke for ten years.

"Will you see if the carriage is there?" the Duke asked aloud. "Then we will carry Richard downstairs."

As Lord Tring turned to leave the room, the Duke added:

"Do not forget that when the High Sheriff sees Gadsby he must have in his hand a duelling pistol which has recently been fired."

"You think of everything, Sir," Lord Tring exclaimed admiringly.

"I am trying to," the Duke replied.

*   *   *

Travelling slowly back along the twisting country roads, the Duke sat with his back to the horses.

As he looked at Richard lying unconscious on the back seat of the carriage, he thought it would have been poetic justice if he had expended his second bullet on Delyth Maulden rather than on himself.

His experience of women told him that while she had appeared calm and unperturbed by what had happened, she was in fact shocked. But at the same time, in her usual selfish manner she was thinking only of herself.

She had lost not one lover but two. Sir Joceline was a rich man, but there was no likelihood of his ever becoming a Duke.

The fact that a duel had been fought over her would not surprise anybody, and, as the Duke had said, would not damage her reputation more than it was damaged already.

At the same time, it was understood that no decent, well-bred woman allowed herself to be the cause of a duel.

Even though sometimes they were involved, the gentlemen would take great care to hide the real cause of a quarrel and would attribute it to anything other than the lady in question.

But with her raffish, improper friends, Lady Delyth would doubtless, the Duke thought grimly, think it another feather in her cap.

However, what was certain at the moment was that nobody of Richard's standing would be likely to offer her marriage.

He wondered if, after all that had happened, she would still try to cling to his offer and declare that they were engaged.

This was in fact one of the reasons why he had decided to take Richard away from Tring Castle.

If Delyth Maulden could come out of the sordid affair with her future assured, she would do so.

Once Richard was home at Kingswood, it would

be easy, the Duke thought, to make sure that she could not come near him, and at the same time to intimate to the Social World that their betrothal had come to an abrupt end.

"Damn her!" he said as he looked at the face of his unconscious heir. "Damn her, and damn all women! Under the skin they are all exactly alike!"

Chapter Two

The Duke and Major Haverington galloped their horses for over a mile before they pulled them up to a slow trot.

It was still very early in the morning, and the sun had not yet dispersed the mist over the river and the dew was heavy on the grass.

Despite the fact that the Duke had not gone to bed until five o'clock he looked amazingly fit.

After bringing Richard back to Kingswood he had sent a groom poste-haste for the local Doctor, and when he arrived there had been the difficult task of locating the bullet and removing it.

Fortunately, Dr. Emerson was a skilled Surgeon. He had served in the Army and was therefore experienced in gun-shot wounds.

"A fraction of an inch lower, Your Grace," he had said when the operation was over, "and there would have been no hope of saving Mr. Richard."

"I have been told you can perform miracles, Emerson," the Duke replied, "and on this occasion I was present at one."

The Doctor, however, did not smile at the compliment.

"We are not yet out of the woods," he said. "Mr. Richard will need very careful nursing, but he is in good health and he has always been so since he was a small boy."

"That is definitely a point in his favour," the Duke remarked drily.

But after everything was over he had found it difficult to sleep, and had lain awake hoping not only that Richard would live but that Delyth would get her just deserts for bringing him to such a pass.

At the same time, when he had related what had happened to Major Haverington while they breakfasted together at seven o'clock, the latter exclaimed:

"You will have difficulty, Nolan, in getting rid of Lady Delyth. After this has happened, more doors will be closed in her face and only marriage will save her."

"Do you imagine that I would allow her to marry Richard?" the Duke asked. "It would be over my dead body!"

The Major did not reply, but both men felt as if the threat of Delyth Maulden hung in the air.

Now, riding over the fields golden with buttercups which seemed to echo the glory of the sun, the Duke said:

"If Richard lives, I will find him a decent wife."

"That is exactly the same tone of voice you used to use, Nolan, whenever you said: 'We will take the enemy position whatever the odds against us!'"

"At least that woman should have cured him of expecting to find happiness with her sort!" the Duke exclaimed savagely.

"However much you may hate her," Major Haverington replied, "you have to admit that she is beautiful."

"It is not the sort of beauty I admire," the Duke retorted.

"Then you are different from every other man in London," the Major said. "Even though I despise her, even though I know exactly how evil her influence can be on younger men, I still have to say that she is beautiful."

"Stop talking about her," the Duke stormed. "You have to help me, Bevil, not only to make sure that

Richard forgets her but also to find somebody to put in her place."

"Are you not being a little premature in your plans for him?"

"I have always believed that the only antidote to one love-affair is another," the Duke replied.

"I suppose that is true," his friend replied. "But when a man loves as wildly and fervently as Richard loves Lady Delyth, it is difficult to divert his interests into another channel."

"It may be hard, but that is what we have to do," the Duke replied sharply. "As soon as he is convalescing, I will invite the right sort of girls to stay."

Major Haverington did not reply.

He was thinking that the Duke was planning out a campaign in his usual manner, considering every detail and leaving nothing to chance.

It amused him to see the Duke back in his old place of authority, plotting, scheming, going into action in a way that was peculiarly his own.

He wondered if it would be as easy for him to win a victory when he was not concerned with soldiers and their duty to destroy the enemy, but with a man and a woman, and with love.

"I know what you are thinking," the Duke said sharply. "And make no mistake, Bevil: in this instance I intend to be the victor."

"I wish you luck," Major Haverington said, "but do not underestimate your adversary."

"Meaning Delyth Maulden?"

"I was really thinking of Richard's feelings," the Major answered. "Delyth may be difficult, but I am certain you will be able to deal with her. What I am finding it impossible to visualise is somebody who could take her place in that wretched boy's affections."

The Duke was silent, then he muttered beneath his breath:

"There must be somebody!"

As he spoke, he was thinking of women he knew, but however beautiful or glamorous they might be, they would none of them be of the slightest use in this particular instance.

To begin with, the majority of them were married, and the rest were widows, sophisticated and certainly on the look-out for another husband, but far too old for Richard and not the type of woman that he wished to see as the future Duchess of Kingswood.

Feeling as if he was following his friend's train of thought, the Major remarked:

"Richard is just twenty-one. What you want to find is a girl of eighteen or nineteen."

"I know," the Duke agreed. "The extraordinary thing is that I cannot remember when I last spoke to a girl of that age, let alone had any knowledge of her personality or character."

He saw that the Major was smiling, and he went on:

"Dammit all, do girls of that age have any character? I have a feeling that most of them when they leave the School-Room are nit-witted."

"They learn quickly enough," the Major said laconically. "And do not forget that the charmers you now find so alluring were once half-baked school-girls, innocent of all the temptations of the wicked world outside."

The Duke was silent.

The Major had spoken jokingly, but he knew that there was truth in what he had said.

At the same time, vaguely, at the back of his mind, he was forming an image of the sort of girl he wanted his heir to marry.

Someone quiet and gentle, sweet and understanding. Someone who would love Richard for himself and not only make him a charming wife but be an admirable mother to his children.

Although the idea of what he wanted presented itself to him, he could not put a face to this creature of his imagination and certainly not a name.

"I have a feeling, Nolan," the Major remarked as he rode beside him, "that you will have to start attending the Balls that will be given during the Season and peer into the Drawing-Rooms at Buckingham Palace when the Débutantes are presented."

The Duke groaned audibly and the Major went on in a more serious tone:

"You know as well as I do that the sort of wife you want for Richard will not be found at Carlton House or in the Royal Pavilion at Brighton, and you certainly will not be introduced to her by a member of White's."

"Stop needling me!" the Duke ordered.

"As it happens, I am speaking the truth," the Major said. "At the same time, I am making you understand that your task is not going to be an easy one."

"I have asked you to help me," the Duke said, "and you are more likely than I am to find the sort of girl I want. You know that if I am thought to be looking round the Marriage-Market, the ambitious Mamas will be onto me like a pack of wolves!"

That was true enough, the Major agreed, for of all the catches in the Matrimonial-World, the most important and the most unlikely ever to be ensnared was the Duke of Kingswood.

But that would not prevent every mother from hoping fondly that he might take a fancy to her particular chick, and the mere hint that the Duke's eye was looking in a particular direction would raise forlorn hopes and undoubtedly ensure that he never had another moment's peace.

"I will tell you what I will do, Nolan," the Major said. "When we go back to London I will talk to my sister. She is extremely sensible and in fact has a daughter of her own coming out next year."

"Perhaps she would do for Richard?" the Duke suggested.

"I doubt it," the Major replied. "Jane is a nice child, but unfortunately she takes after her father and is no beauty."

"I wonder if Richard would obey me if I tried to pressurise him into marriage," the Duke remarked reflectively. "After all, if his father were still alive, an alliance would doubtless have been arranged by now."

"The modern young woman has become very independent," the Major replied. "Perhaps it is the result of the war. The Earl of Thame was telling me only a month ago that his eldest daughter refused point blank a most advantageous marriage, and nothing he could say would alter her decision."

The Duke laughed.

"Thame said to me," the Major went on, " 'In my grandfather's and indeed in my father's time, she would have been whipped and kept on bread and water, until she agreed to do as she was told, but nowadays the girls do as they like!' "

"As you say, it must be the war," the Duke replied, "but I always understood that a girl obeyed her parents and any rebellious thoughts were soon crushed out of her."

"You must certainly meet my niece," the Major said with a laugh. "Jane is a fearless rider to hounds, as are all my sister's children, and if they are brave in one way they are brave in another: I have heard her defy her father a dozen times."

"You had better find someone more pliable," the Duke said briefly. "I am relying on you, Bevil. Since Richard will take a long time to get back on his feet, he will not be able to escape either the attentions or the attractions of anyone you provide for him."

"Really, Nolan, you do give me the most impossible tasks!" Major Haverington complained. "I remember you were just the same when we reached France and there was no food and the transport-wagons were miles behind."

"I seem to recall that after a most unmilitary protest to your Commanding-Officer," the Duke said, "you did as you were told and came back from a forage with quite a number of edible animals."

"I nearly lost my life when I commandeered them from the farmer to whom they belonged," Major Haverington retorted. "But fortunately, unlike the French, the English paid for what they took; otherwise I should certainly not be talking to you now!"

"What I am pointing out is that whatever methods you used, you were successful," the Duke said.

"Buying a few old cows and some fat pigs is rather different from producing a wife for Richard," the Major replied; "and let me tell you here and now, you are not going to get what you require."

"Why should you say that?"

"Because you are asking the impossible!"

"What do you mean?"

"I mean that you want a girl who is innocent, pure, attractive, and clever, to make Richard forget a witch who has cast a spell both on his heart and on his mind."

"Quite an acceptable summary of my requirements," the Duke said briefly. "At least you know what is required."

"Damn you, Nolan, find her yourself!" Bevil Haverington replied.

As he spoke he spurred his horse and moved ahead, while the Duke, with a smile, followed him.

The smile, however, was undoubtedly cynical, for the Duke was well aware that he was in fact asking the impossible.

Even if Richard despised or even loathed Delyth for the way in which she had behaved, that was not to say he would not still yearn after her or that her hold on him would be weakened to the point when he no longer wished to see her.

"He will get over her in time," the Duke told himself.

But he was in fact not as confident as he might have been where somebody else was concerned.

Richard, who had been brought up by a doting mother and father, was absurdly idealistic.

The Duke was sure that he wrote poetry for

Delyth and would have compared her in his mind not only with Aphrodite but with every fair goddess dwelling on Olympus.

There was no denying that she was witty as well as beautiful, talented, and intelligent.

It was just unfortunate that the picture was spoilt by a temperament that was as lustful as any man's, and that purity, of either mind or body, was a word not included in her particular vocabulary.

"Delyth is not the only woman in the world," the Duke said when he caught up with the Major.

"Thank God for that!" was the fervent reply.

The two friends rode on until, as the sun rose and it grew warmer, they turned their horses for home.

They were still a long way from Kingswood when they saw it silhouetted on the horizon, its roofs and towers gleaming in the sunshine, and the trees, vivid with the green of spring, circling it like a jewel.

"I have often thought," the Major remarked as he looked at it, "that Kingswood is the most beautiful house in the whole country."

"I agree with you," the Duke replied, "but then I presume I am prejudiced."

"It is too big for one man alone," the Major went on. "It should be filled with children—your children, Nolan."

The Duke rode on without speaking, and his friend wondered, as he had wondered so often before, what was the secret which had obviously erected a barrier between him and the women who chased after him so ardently.

'It is not Richard whom we should be worrying about, but Nolan,' the Major thought. 'He would surely be happier if he were married.'

His own thoughts startled him because he was presupposing that the Duke was not happy. Yet, how could he be anything else, in view not only of his great possessions but of his personal attributes as a man?

There was no-one who rode better, who could drive a four-in-hand with more expertise, who was a better shot with a pistol, or who could fence on equal terms with the professionals.

Besides all this, the Major knew, although it was an interest he could not share with his friend, that the Duke was a great reader.

Even on the battle-field he had always carried with him a supply of books, and the Major had an idea that when he wanted to escape from the horrors of war, he could do so because he was concentrating on a book which carried his mind away from present reality.

'There must be a woman who can share such a taste with him,' the Major thought.

But even if there was, there was no use in speaking of it. To do so would result in the Duke immediately retreating into his shell, and there was a reserve about him which even his closest friends could not penetrate.

They rode on a little farther, talking about the spring crops, and noting the partridges which had mated and the teal swimming in twos on the stream which ran along the foot of the meadow over which they were riding.

They neared the Home Farm and the Duke remarked:

"I have a good man at the farm now. He is raising a better herd of Jerseys for the house than we have had for a very long time."

"I would like to see them," the Major said.

"We will go there tomorrow," the Duke promised. "I think we ought to return now and see how Richard is progressing."

"Yes, of course," the Major agreed. "What time is the Doctor coming?"

"He said about nine o'clock," the Duke replied.

There was no doubt from the way he spoke that he was perturbed about the boy, and the Major hoped for the Duke's sake that Richard would survive.

It had been a shock when the Duke told him what had happened. At the same time, he had not been surprised.

Delyth Maulden's devastating effect on young men had been certain, sooner or later, to end in tragedy.

"Tomorrow I will also show you the mares I have in foal . . ." the Duke was saying.

Then unexpectedly from a barn on the outskirts of the farm a woman came running towards them.

She was waving her arms as if to attract their attention, and the Duke reined in his horse, as did the Major.

As she came nearer, they saw that she was very young and had fair hair the colour of sunshine.

She was obviously a peasant or a milk-maid, for the gown she wore was faded and the skirt was patched.

"I wonder who this is," the Duke said as she came nearer.

When she reached the side of his horse she was breathless and for a moment found it impossible to speak.

Then as both the Duke and the Major waited, she said earnestly:

"Help . . . me! Please . . . help me!"

"What is the matter?" the Duke asked.

As the girl, for she was nothing more, spoke, the Major was aware that she was exceptionally pretty.

Her eyes were very large in a small pointed face, and surprisingly, although her hair was fair, her eyelashes were dark, while her eyes, instead of being blue as might have been expected, were the colour of a cloudy sky.

At least that was what they appeared, but it might have been because she was obviously frightened and the pupils were dilated.

"What has happened to you?" the Duke asked.

"It is my . . . father," she said with a gasp. "He is ill . . . unconscious. I am afraid . . . he may have suffered a . . . stroke!"

The Major noticed that the words were spoken in an educated voice, which he had certainly not expected from the shabby appearance of the speaker.

"Where is your father?" the Duke asked.

"In the barn," the girl replied. "It is where we ... slept last ... night."

"Then let us go and see what we can do for him," the Duke suggested.

He moved his horse forward and the girl walked beside him, still struggling to get her breath.

The Major, riding behind, realised that she was very slender and moved with a grace that was unmistakable.

'She is certainly not a gypsy,' he thought to himself; 'but who else would wander about the countryside, sleeping in a barn?'

He thought her hair, as she walked beside the Duke, was a colour that most women would envy; it was that which Opera-dancers unsuccessfully tried to achieve with a dye.

It was not far to the barn, and the girl ran ahead of the Duke to pull the door, which was ajar, open a little wider.

The Duke dismounted, handed the reins of his horse to the Major, and walked through the door.

The barn had originally held the winter's hay, but now there was only a small pile of it left and that was in a corner where the girl was already bending over the body of a man.

The Duke joined her.

He looked down and saw, to his surprise, a distinguished-looking man with white hair and fine, clear-cut features. He was wearing a threadbare black coat and at his neck were the two white muslin bands which proclaimed him as being a Parson.

His eyes were shut and his face was so pale that at first the Duke thought he was dead.

Then as he felt for his pulse, as he had done for Richard last night, he found that there was a very faint beat, so faint that at first he thought it was nonexistent.

"He is ... alive?"

The three words were spoken in such a tone of desperate anxiety that the Duke felt relieved that he could reply:

"Yes, he is alive, but I think you are right—he may have had a stroke."

The girl clasped her fingers together as if in an effort at self-control.

"What ... can I ... do?" she asked. "Where can I ... find a ... Doctor for him?"

"As it happens," the Duke replied, "a Doctor is calling at my house in less than an hour's time."

"Then could you ... ask him to ... see my ... father?"

"I think it would be best," the Duke replied, "if your father was taken to a more congenial place than this."

The girl's eyes widened. Then she said:

"I am ... afraid we have ... no money."

"I am not asking you to pay," the Duke replied, with a faint smile on his lips. "You had better leave everything in my hands."

He turned to walk back the way he had come, and after a second's pause the girl followed him.

"What are you ... going to do?" she asked.

"I am going over to the farm," the Duke replied, "to ask if the farmer will bring your father to my house in a wagon. I expect you will wish to accompany him, and the best way to save him from being jolted would be for you to sit on the floor of the wagon and hold his head in your lap."

"I will do ... that," the girl answered breathlessly. "Thank you! Thank you ... very much!"

The Duke reached the door of the barn, then he stopped and looked at her.

"What is your name?" he enquired.

"Calvine," she answered. "My father is the Reverend Aaron Calvine, and we come from ... Northumberland."

The Duke raised his eye-brows but made no

comment. He merely swung himself onto his horse, and as he picked up the reins he said:

"Expect the wagon to come for you within the next fifteen minutes. I will see you later."

He rode away and the Major followed him to ask:

"What has happened? Who is that attractive young woman?"

"Her father is a Parson and he has undoubtedly had a stroke. I thought at first he was dead."

"A Parson!" the Major exclaimed. "What was he doing in one of your barns?"

"I have no idea," the Duke replied, "but doubtless we shall be told in due course the story of why they are so far from home."

"And where is that?" the Major asked.

"Northumberland," the Duke replied.

"I believe you are being deliberately mysterious!" the Major said accusingly.

"I am merely relating all I know myself," the Duke replied. "As the Parson appeared to be on the point of death, it was hardly a moment to subject his daughter to a catechism."

"It seems extraordinary to me," the Major said. "If they live in Northumberland, what on earth are they doing here?"

The Duke did not reply, because they had reached the yard of the farm.

As soon as they clattered into it the farmer appeared, obviously pleased and gratified to see his employer.

"Good-marnin', Your Grace. Oi were a-hoping ye'd call."

"This is not exactly a social visit, Telford," the Duke replied. "I have just found a very ill man in one of your barns."

"A man?" the farmer echoed. "If it be one o' they pesky gypsies, Your Grace, Oi'll take a pitch-fork to 'e!"

"No, he is no gypsy, but a Parson, who I think has suffered a stroke."

The Duke saw the astonishment in the farmer's face and went on:

"Get a wagon and convey him to the house. A Doctor will be calling on me in the next twenty minutes and I wish to see what he can do to help the gentleman."

"Tha's good o' Your Grace," the farmer said, "but he'd no roight to be a-sleeping in me barn, an' Oi can't think why the dogs didn't hear 'e."

"Whatever his reasons, he is obviously extremely ill," the Duke said. "I have told his daughter, who is with him, that you will bring him over to the house as quickly as possible."

"Oi'll do that, Your Grace, but they'd no roight to be there, an' tha's a fact!"

"I shall be waiting for you," the Duke said briefly, and rode away to prevent any further argument.

He galloped home at such a speed that it was impossible for the Major to question him further.

When they arrived at Kingswood, the grooms were waiting outside the front door to take the horses and there were footmen on the steps.

In the Great Hall the Duke handed his hat and whip to the Butler, saying:

"There is a wagon arriving here in a short space of time, Bateman, carrying an extremely ill man. I want Dr. Emerson to see him when he arrives, so instruct Mrs. Newall to have a bed-room prepared for another patient."

"Very good, Your Grace, I'll tell Mrs. Newall right away."

The Duke walked across the Hall.

Then as he was turning towards the Library a sudden thought struck him and he turned back to say:

"There is a young woman with the sick man—his daughter. Tell Mrs. Newall that two rooms will be required."

"Very good, Your Grace."

The Duke walked into the Library.

"It never rains, but it pours!" he remarked.

"First Richard, and now a wandering Parson. I wonder who will be the third casualty."

"Good Lord, Nolan! Two is enough!" the Major exclaimed. "The house will become a Hospital if you are not careful."

"I could not leave the Parson to die unattended in an empty barn," the Duke replied, as if he was excusing himself.

"No, of course not," the Major said. "At the same time, it was generous of you to bring him here."

"I could hardly say that there was not enough room," the Duke replied with a twist of his lips.

Two footmen appeared with a tray on which there was a silver coffee-pot and two large cups.

Unlike his contemporaries who invariably drank brandy or wine after they had been riding, the Duke preferred coffee and the Major followed his example.

Holding his cup in his hand, the Duke walked to the window to look out at the lake, which glittered golden in the sunshine.

"I have a feeling, Bevil," he said, "that yesterday you were thinking it was rather quiet here and that nothing ever happens in the country. Well, your thoughts have certainly been confounded in the last twenty-four hours."

"That is true," the Major agreed. "But I suspect, Nolan, that however tragic Richard's predicament may be, you are quite enjoying the challenge it affords you."

" 'Challenge' is the right word," the Duke agreed. "It is a challenge, and now I am also wondering how I may be involved in taking on another seriously ill man."

As he spoke, the door opened and a flunkey announced:

"Dr. Emerson, Your Grace!"

The Duke turned with his hand outstretched.

"Good-morning, Doctor. I am glad to see you. Have you had a chance yet to examine your patient?"

"Not yet, Your Grace."

The Doctor was a middle-aged man who had

treated the Wood family ever since he had first come
to the neighbourhood.

He knew that Richard Wood was the Duke's
heir presumptive and that if he died, the title and
the estate would pass to another cousin, whom all the
family disliked.

He therefore said, with an effort to create opti-
mism:

"I'm sure he's been well looked after by Hawkins, who is a better Nurse than anyone I could
provide."

"Hawkins is excellent in that capacity," the Duke
agreed. "He told me before I went riding that Richard
had passed a peaceful night and he thought he was
breathing a little easier."

"That's good news, Your Grace!" the Doctor
exclaimed. "I'll go up and examine him, then bring
you a report."

"When you have finished with Richard, I have
another patient for you to see," the Duke said.

Dr. Emerson raised his eye-brows.

"Another?"

"Yes. I found a Parson in one of the barns on
the farm, who appears to have suffered a stroke."

"A Parson?"

It was a question and a puzzled one.

"Nobody knows him," the Duke said quickly.
"In fact his daughter tells me that they come from
Northumberland."

"Now I know who you are talking about," Dr.
Emerson replied. "One of my patients told me that
she had heard there was a Preacher in the neighbourhood and asked if he could come and pray with
her."

He paused, then as if in explanation he added:

"I will not bore Your Grace with the story of the
long feud that exists between the old lady in question
and our local Vicar. She will not allow him to cross
her threshold, yet she thinks she requires solace for
her soul."

"Then you can tell your patient," the Duke said,

"that the Preacher is unlikely to be able to help her at the moment. But you shall judge for yourself."

"I'll ask Bateman to let me know when he arrives," the Doctor said. "It was kind of you to bring him here."

"As I have just said to my friend Major Haverington, I cannot complain that there is not enough room," the Duke answered.

The Doctor laughed.

"No, indeed. You could quite easily house an Army Corps. I only wish we'd had a Hospital of the same size in France."

*   *   *

It was nearly luncheon-time when the Duke and Major Haverington met again in the Library.

The Duke had not only received a report from Dr. Emerson regarding the two patients who were in the house, but he had also dealt with a large correspondence brought to him by his secretary, and listened to a number of requests from the Major-Domo concerning repairs and decorations that were necessary in the house.

It had in fact been a full morning, and he felt he was entitled to a glass of champagne, which the Butler poured out for him.

"Well, Bevil, what have you found to do?" he enquired.

The Major was just about to answer him when the Butler asked in a respectful voice:

"Excuse me asking, Your Grace, but I was not sure where you would wish the young lady to have luncheon."

For a moment the Duke found it difficult to think of whom he was speaking.

Then he realised that he was referring to the daughter of the Reverend Aaron Calvine, and he noted with faint amusement that the Butler, who was an extremely perceptive man when it came to putting people in their right categories, referred to Miss Calvine as a "lady."

The Duke hesitated before he replied with a twinkle in his eyes:

"Ask Miss Calvine to have luncheon with us in the Dining-Room."

"Very good, Your Grace."

Bateman left the room and the Major exclaimed:

"The Dining-Room? Surely that is unexpected?"

"Why not?" the Duke replied. "You are bursting with curiosity, and since neither I nor the Doctor can tell you all you wish to know, you can ask her for yourself."

"The Dining-Room!" the Major repeated, thinking of the shabby appearance of the girl who had run to them for their help.

"A guest is always a guest," the Duke said blithely. "Even my father invited the local Vicar to dinner once a year."

"My father still does the same," Major Haverington said with a laugh, "and an extremely boring meal it usually turns out to be!"

"It is undoubtedly a traditional duty," the Duke said, "and therefore we must not shirk ours where the Parson's daughter is concerned."

He poured himself another glass of champagne, and he thought, as the Major followed his example, that they both had some reason to be curious about the travelling Preacher.

The Duke remembered such men moving about the countryside when he was a boy.

They usually appeared at the local races and horse-fairs, declaiming against the sins of those who were gaming and threatening the fires of hell as a punishment for those who did not listen.

He remembered being fascinated by the way their voices were raised in a kind of rapture that excited those who listened.

Sometimes the exhortation was followed by a hymn, after which there would invariably be a collection, and most of the crowd who had pretended to listen would quickly drift away.

The Duke supposed that that was how the Parson

and his daughter must live, and he thought that their congregations could not have been very generous, because the girl had said they had no money.

The door opened and Bateman announced:

"Miss Calvine, Your Grace!"

She was still wearing the shabby, patched gown that she had worn early in the morning, but now there was a clean white collar round her neck which gave her the appearance of a Quaker.

Her shining hair was neatly gathered into a bun at the back of her head, and her eyes, which the Major now realised were the colour of the morning mist, were wide and apprehensive in her pale face.

She looked at the Duke a little anxiously, then curtseyed with the grace that the Major had noticed when she had walked ahead of him.

"I was told," she said in a quiet little voice, "that I was to have luncheon with . . . Your Grace."

There was a pause before the last two words, and it was obvious that when she had learnt who her host was she had been surprised.

"I am delighted to hear from the Doctor that your father is none the worse for the journey here," the Duke said.

"The Doctor confirmed that Papa has in fact had a stroke and is in a coma."

"You can trust Dr. Emerson to do what is right for him," the Duke reassured her. "May I offer you a glass of champagne?"

"No . . . thank you."

"You are quite sure? This morning must have been a shock, and a glass of wine will do you good."

"It is . . . kind of you . . . but I very seldom drink . . . wine, and I have not had . . . anything to eat today."

It struck the Duke from the way she spoke that she had eaten little the day before, and he knew she was being sensible in refusing the champagne.

He was about to suggest that she might like another sort of drink, but then luncheon was announced.

Without being told to do so, Miss Calvine walked beside the Duke down the wide corridor which crossed the Hall and continued on the other side towards the Dining-Room.

She did not speak, but he noted that she looked at the pictures, and he thought it would be hard for anyone, let alone a poverty-stricken Parson's daughter, not to be impressed.

In the Dining-Room the Duke sat at the head of the table, with his latest guest on his right and Major Haverington on his left.

The Duke, who had seen starvation in Portugal and in the last years of the war in the villages of France, knew by the sharpness of the girl's chin-bone and the thinness of her wrists that she was under-nourished.

He also noticed that she ate slowly and deliberately, taking minute portions of each course, as if she was well aware that it would be harmful for her to eat very much.

In fact, before the meal was finished it was obvious that it was impossible for her to consume more.

But she drew no attention to the fact or to herself, but merely answered the questions she was asked in the soft, cultured voice which had struck the Major as being so unexpected the first time she had spoken.

"You have come all the way from Northumberland on foot?" the Duke asked.

"Yes, Your Grace. My father wished to preach to those who would hear him and to pray for those who were ill."

"He has no Parish of his own?"

"Quite a large one when we lived in Huntingford."

"Then why did your father leave?" the Duke enquired.

He felt that in a way he was taking an unfair advantage in forcing her to speak about herself. At the same time, he knew that if he did not ask the questions, the Major would.

"When my mother died," Miss Calvine said in a low voice, "my father could not bear to stay any longer in the house where they had been so happy together. He felt he had a call to help the people outside the Parish. I could not let him go alone, so I went with him."

"It must have been a difficult thing for you to do," the Duke said.

"Not really," Miss Calvine replied. "I love him, and we have always been happy together."

"It seems strange," the Major interposed, "that your father should wish to do such a thing."

"Papa was always unpredictable," Miss Calvine replied, "but he is a scholar, and all he read told him that those who inspired others invariably felt the need to go into the wilderness at some time or other."

The Duke looked at her questioningly.

"The wilderness?"

"That is only a figure of speech, Your Grace," she replied. "Jesus fasted for forty days and forty nights in the wilderness, and Buddha left his home and wandered for many years until he found enlightenment. Mohammed went on a pilgrimage, and so did every Spiritual Leader of whom one has ever heard."

"Does your father think he is a Leader in some way?" Major Haverington asked incredulously.

"I think he does," Miss Calvine answered, "but then everyone who is consumed by faith believes that they must carry their message to those who are ignorant."

The Duke was astonished by the way she spoke.

Then, after another course had been taken round the table, he asked:

"You told me that your father's name is Aaron, which is somewhat unusual. May I enquire what is your Christian name?"

"I think you will find that unusual too," Miss Calvine said with a smile. "It is Benedicta."

"I have never heard of it before!" the Major ejaculated.

"I was expected to be a boy," she explained, "and was to be called Benedict. My father had a special feeling for the Saint of that name. When I was disappointingly a girl, he merely added an 'a' to the name he had chosen."

The Duke smiled, then he said:

"As Benedict means 'blessed,' you certainly have something to live up to."

"I know," Benedicta replied, "and I find it somewhat intimidating."

As luncheon progressed, the Duke and the Major learnt, by asking undeniably curious questions, that the Parish in Huntingford had been the gift of Benedicta's grandfather.

"Surely," the Duke exclaimed, "your grandfather must have wished to prevent you from setting off on this strange journey with your father, with apparently no money for your food or for anything else?"

"Papa believed that God would provide us with all that was necessary," Benedicta replied.

Then she added with a touch of humour in her voice:

"And indeed He has, except when it comes to my gowns!"

The Duke laughed as if he could not help himself.

"Perhaps you come in the same category as 'the lilies of the field,'" he answered, "and are expected to provide your own raiment."

"That is something I have often thought myself," Benedicta agreed. "I am not complaining, but I do feel slightly out-of-place in this wonderful house."

She looked round her as she spoke, and then she added:

"Your pictures take my breath away! Might I be allowed to look at them when I am not caring for Papa?"

"I should be delighted to show you the best of them myself," the Duke said.

"But you have not answered the question," the Major said impulsively. "Why did your grandfather let you leave Huntingford?"

There was a little pause before Benedicta said:

"I am afraid my father and grandfather do not see eye to eye. He is very orthodox and he did not like the way Papa took the Services, and he actively disliked his sermons."

There was a faint smile on her lips as she added:

"In the end, he even left the Church before Papa preached!"

"That is something I have often wanted to do myself!" the Major exclaimed.

"I think that after Mama died," Benedicta went on, "if Papa had not left, my grandfather would have found some way of throwing him out of the Parish."

"So you just walked out?" the Duke asked.

"Papa decided one night that we would go away, and we left the next morning."

"You did indeed walk out!" the Duke exclaimed.

"It was like starting a new life," Benedicta said, "or opening the pages of a new book. We laid aside the past and set off into the future."

There was something wistful about the way she spoke.

The Duke, who was unusually perceptive, thought that she was thinking not of the material luxuries she was leaving behind but perhaps the memory of her mother and the friends she must have had in the village and in the County.

Having had a chance to look at her, he realised that she was in fact not pretty, as the Major had said, but lovely in a different way from any other woman he had seen before.

At first her face had seemed so pale and peaked that he had not thought of her as anything but a pleasant-looking young girl.

But after she had eaten and the colour had come back into her cheeks and the sparkle into her eyes, he saw that it was only hunger and perhaps shock that had made her look drawn and stricken.

Now she was talking to him quite naturally, with her lips curved in a smile, and he thought she had an unusual fascination besides an expression that was almost spiritual.

Despite her reference to her shabbiness, he wondered how any other woman of his acquaintance would have carried off her threadbare, patched gown without being so uncomfortably conscious of it that she would have communicated the feeling both to himself and to the Major.

As it was, as Benedicta talked she might, for all the difference it made, have been attired in the very latest fashion.

'Perhaps she thinks it is a sin to think too much about herself,' the Duke thought a little sardonically.

But then he knew that Benedicta's behaviour was entirely natural and came not only from a lack of self-consciousness but also from a pride and what was obviously good breeding.

He found himself as curious as the Major had been to know more about her.

"What is the name of your grandfather?" he asked.

"Marlow," she replied, "but in Huntingford they always refer to him as 'the Squire.'"

"That is what they call my father," the Major said.

"I think it is rather a nice title," Benedicta said with a smile, "for it means that the people you employ and those who are your tenants look up to you as if you are a father-figure."

"Your grandfather does not appear to have looked after you very well," the Duke commented.

"He would have done so if I had not left with my father," Benedicta replied, "but I promised . . ."

She stopped suddenly, as if she felt that she was talking too intimately to strangers, and the Duke felt that both he and the Major had been unfair in almost forcing her to reveal her private life.

Tactfully, with a charm that he could exert when he pleased, the Duke began to talk about his pictures, and he knew by the wide-eyed manner in which she listened to him that Benedicta was genuinely interested.

When luncheon was over they moved from the Dining-Room towards the Library, but when they reached the Hall she stopped.

"I must go to Papa," she said. "Thank you very much for inviting me to luncheon with Your Grace."

"We were delighted to have you," the Duke said, "and I hope you will also dine with us."

He was surprised when Benedicta hesitated.

His eyes were on her face and he knew that something perturbed her. Then after a moment she said:

"It is very kind of Your Grace, but I feel that as dinner is a more formal meal . . . I . . . I should be somewhat . . . out-of-place."

The Duke knew she was speaking of her appearance, and he replied:

"The Major and I will be alone, and we should be very disappointed if you refuse to join us. As you have raised the point, you will find us quite informal."

He smiled as he spoke, and after a second she smiled faintly in response, then curtseyed.

"Your Grace is more . . . kind than I can possibly . . . express," she said, "and . . . thank you . . . again!"

She turned towards the stairs as she spoke, and the Duke walked into the Library.

The Major followed him and closed the door.

"Talk about manna from Heaven!" he exclaimed. "Your prayers are answered! After this I will always believe in miracles!"

"What are you talking about?" the Duke enquired.

"Benedicta!"

"What about her?"

"You were searching for her—or rather you instructed me to do so—and out of the sky she appeared. What more can you ask?"

The Duke, who had been walking towards the

desk in the centre of the room, stood still and stared at his friend.

"Can you really be suggesting . . . ?"

"Why not?" the Major answered before he could finish the sentence. "She is lovely, she is obviously pure and innocent, and she is very different in every possible way from Delyth Maulden. What is more—which is something you did not specify—she is a lady!"

There was silence for a moment, then the Duke laughed.

"My dear Bevil, I believe you are right! You call it manna from Heaven, and that is exactly what it is!"

Chapter Three

The Duke sent for Mrs. Newall.

She stood in the Library with her hands folded over her black silk apron, her chatelaine glinting in the sunlight coming through the long windows.

"I want your help, Mrs. Newall."

The Duke was seated at the huge rosewood writing-desk which stood in the centre of the room and which had been used by the owners of Kingswood for many generations.

He knew that Mrs. Newall was an extremely efficient Housekeeper and had not only the well-being of the house at heart, but also that of the family.

All the older servants at Kingswood spoke as if the house and the estate, and everything that appertained to them, were part of themselves.

In fact, since he had inherited, the Duke had often thought that the whole place was like one big family, and he intended to keep it that way.

"I'll be glad, Your Grace, to do anything that's in my power," Mrs. Newall said in her well-modulated voice.

"It concerns Miss Calvine," the Duke said.

He paused, knowing that Mrs. Newall was listening attentively.

"It appears," he went on, "that it will be a long time before Miss Calvine's father can be restored to health; and as I know they have no money, I am concerned with what she has to wear while staying here."

He saw a responsive expression on Mrs. Newall's face but she did not speak, and he continued:

"It would, of course, be incorrect for me to provide a young woman with clothes, even though I am prepared to do so, but I was thinking that perhaps you could do something about her appearance."

"I understand, Your Grace, from the housemaid who is looking after Miss Calvine," Mrs. Newall said, "that she's nothing with her except a few meagre necessities which she carries in a small bag."

"That is what I suspected," the Duke replied, "considering the fact that they walked from Northumberland!"

"One can hardly credit, Your Grace, that such a fragile young lady as Miss Calvine could have survived such an experience."

"She must be stronger than she looks," the Duke answered, "but obviously her gown and doubtless her shoes have suffered."

"They have indeed, Your Grace!" Mrs. Newall said, suddenly garrulous on the subject. "How Miss Calvine can walk at all, seeing the soles of her shoes are worn through to the bare flesh, I'll never know!"

"Then what can we do about it, Mrs. Newall?" the Duke asked.

"It had crossed my mind," Mrs. Newall replied, "that Miss Calvine's feet might be the same size as those of Her late Grace. There are quite a number of her possessions here, which have been moved upstairs."

Mrs. Newall was obviously thinking as she spoke, because she hesitated for a moment before going on:

"I think too there're some slippers which belonged to Lady Emmeline when she was a girl."

"And perhaps some gowns?" the Duke suggested.

Mrs. Newall shook her head.

"I think not, Your Grace. If there were, they'd be sadly out-of-date; and perhaps you remember that

Lady Emmeline was on the large side, even when she was in her teens."

The Duke nodded.

Lady Emmeline had always been large in build and had put on weight after child-bearing.

"What I've got, Your Grace," Mrs. Newall continued, "is some rolls of material. Her Grace often bought muslins and silks when she was in London, intending to have simple gowns made by her lady's-maid."

"Then that will solve our problem," the Duke said. "I do no think Miss Calvine could refuse material that is obviously not being used, and also would not feel that we were treating her as an object of charity."

"I'm sure the young lady wouldn't feel like that, Your Grace," Mrs. Newall protested. "She's no airs and graces about her and is exceedingly grateful for anything that's done to help her and her father."

"Then I will leave these matters in your capable hands, Mrs. Newall," the Duke said. "If there are things you want to buy for Miss Calvine, of course do so, but perhaps it would be more tactful to let her think they come from your store of unwanted goods."

Mrs. Newall gave the Duke a look of understanding, and promising once again to do her best, she curtseyed and left the Library.

After she had gone, the Duke sent for Hawkins.

He had already spoken to his valet about the nursing of the two invalids and Hawkins had promised to plan everything carefully and let the Duke know how it was to be done.

He came hurrying into the Library, moving smartly, with his shoulders back, as if he were still in uniform.

He was a small, wiry little man, who was possessed of quite extraordinary physical strength and also an endurance which came, the Duke had always thought, from a determination that almost echoed his own.

"Well, Hawkins," he asked, "what have you arranged?"

"I thinks everything'll be to your satisfaction, Your Grace," Hawkins replied. "Mr. Richard's valet and I will take turns in looking after him, and I've found that one of the footmen, Jackson by name, is interested in nursing and wishes to help me with the Reverend gentleman."

Hawkins drew breath and added:

"Of course the young lady, Sir, desires to do everything she can for her father."

"She is not to do too much," the Duke said firmly. "Nursing a heavy man who is unconscious requires a strength that no woman should be expected to have, let alone somebody so frail as Miss Calvine."

"I understand that, Your Grace," Hawkins said in a slightly reproachful tone, as if he thought the Duke had misjudged him.

"Then what have you arranged?"

"Jackson'll sleep across the passage from the Reverend gentleman and be on call at night, but the young lady insists that as her room communicates with that of her father, she'll also be listening for him."

The Duke frowned, and it seemed as if he was about to argue about this arrangement, but then he said:

"Is the Reverend gentleman likely to be restless?"

"Not at the moment, Your Grace. Of course one never knows with a coma. He may come out of it at any time."

"Then Miss Calvine is not to be over-fatigued in what nursing she has to do," the Duke ordered. "And there is another thing, Hawkins."

"Yes, Your Grace?"

"As soon as Mr. Richard is conscious, I would like Miss Calvine, if she is agreeable, to take some part in nursing him."

He saw that the valet looked surprised, and he went on:

"She can read to him, talk to him, and keep him amused in a way which, without disparaging your efforts, would be, I am sure, extremely beneficial."

"Yes, of course, Your Grace, I understand."

When Hawkins left the room there had been a faint smile on the Duke's face, as if he felt he had laid his plans carefully.

He had in fact responded immediately to Major Haverington's suggestion that Benedicta was what they were looking for as a young woman to interest Richard.

Last night when she dined with them he had been extremely struck not only by her looks but also by her intelligence.

It was a long time since he had conversed with a young woman who was not trying to flirt with him or in some way draw his attention to herself as a woman.

Benedicta spoke both to him and to Major Haverington with a frankness and at the same time an impersonal interest that she might have accorded to her father.

In a way, to the Duke it was a sobering thought that they must seem quite old to her, for he had discovered that she was only just nineteen.

At the same time, her knowledge, the way she phrased her sentences, and the manner in which she was prepared to discuss subjects which were not within the usual range for a young woman surprised and, if he was honest, intrigued him.

He soon learnt that the Reverend Aaron Calvine was in fact a scholar of some distinction.

At Oxford he had taken Honours in Classics and had written some short treatises on the Scriptures which had been published by an ecclesiastical firm in London.

They had made no money, but, the Duke learnt, they had brought the author letters from Clerics and other scholars all over the country.

"Why did your father not go on writing?" he asked Benedicta.

"He felt it was too impersonal," she replied. "He believes that those who are in trouble need the human touch, and that is what he tries to give them."

The Duke found that such an answer was refreshingly stimulating to his mind, and he thought when dinner was finished that their conversation had been on a very much higher plane than he remembered ever having had at any meal, either at Kingswood or in London.

As dinner finished, Benedicta asked:

"Ought I to withdraw, Your Grace, and leave you and Major Haverington to your port?"

She spoke as unaffectedly as a child might have done, and the Duke smiled as he replied:

"Neither the Major nor I are heavy drinkers of port and we would like you to stay with us a little while longer, unless you are bored with our company."

"I could never be that," Benedicta replied. "It has been very exciting for me to dine here tonight with you, and in such magnificent surroundings."

"I have not forgotten that I promised to show you my pictures," the Duke said. "And you must tell me if there is anything else you would like to do."

"There is ... one thing I would ... like," Benedicta said, "if you will ... forgive me for ... asking for it."

"What is that?" he enquired.

"If I am very, very careful with them, which indeed I would be," Benedicta said, "may I ... borrow some of your ... books?"

"But of course!" the Duke replied. "My Library is at your disposal."

She gave a sigh of sheer relief and he understood that she had been afraid he might refuse her request.

"It will be so wonderful to have books to read again," she said. "The only thing we could carry with us on our travels was Papa's Bible, and I am beginning to think I know it by heart."

"Then I can certainly offer you some new horizons

in the literary field," the Duke said with a smile. "Do you read French?"

"I am better at Latin," Benedicta answered. "Papa taught me, and also a little Greek."

The Duke's eyes twinkled.

"I think you will find that both the Latin and the Greek books in the Library are even more heavy than the Bible. I am beginning to think, Miss Calvine, that there are important gaps in your education: they come under the heading of—'Frivolous Entertainment.'"

She looked at him for a moment in surprise, then she realised that he was teasing her, and she replied:

"You will find I am a very eager student of that subject, and of a great many others."

She gave an exclamation and put out her hands.

"There is a whole world of knowledge in this house, and I have been telling myself all day how very grateful I am to be here."

She spoke spontaneously, then as if she rebuked herself for being selfish she added:

"But I am really very, very grateful that Papa has been brought to a place where he is ... comfortable and can be ... looked after."

"It is fortunate that you saw us," the Duke remarked.

"I was praying for help," Benedicta said simply, "then there you were, riding across the fields in the sunlight!"

There was something very moving in the way she spoke, and the Duke could not help thinking that the Major had been right when he had referred to her as an answer to their prayers.

Somewhere from the mists of the past a phrase came to his mind and he spoke it aloud:

"I have always been told that God moves in a mysterious way."

He spoke half-mockingly, half-cynically, not really wanting to believe that what had happened was anything but a coincidence and not due to any supernatural cause.

"But of course He does!" Benedicta replied. "And Papa would think it very foolish of me to have doubted for one moment that help would come when it was necessary."

The Duke knew that Major Haverington was thinking that just as they had thought Benedicta was manna from Heaven, that is what they had been to her.

When later she had left them and they were alone in the Library, the Major said:

"That is a very unusual young woman, Nolan. If you ask me, she is far too intelligent for Richard."

"When he is well enough to talk to her," the Duke said, "I will give her a hint that she must not frighten him by being too erudite."

"If Richard, like most of the other young Bucks, has even read a serious book since he left College, I shall be surprised."

"Perhaps you will be," the Duke retorted enigmatically, wanting to defend his heir even while he thought that doubtless the Major was right.

During the night he told himself that while it seemed a preposterous idea to find a wife for Richard, the presence of someone of his own age would doubtless make his convalescence quicker than it would be otherwise.

He wondered what Richard's tastes were, apart, of course, from Delyth Maulden.

He personally had never spoken to him about anything except horses and other sporting interests.

It was Richard's mother who had told him that he was noble and idealistic and knew little of the Social World.

Mothers, the Duke thought, were not unnaturally prejudiced in the favour of their offspring, and he wondered now what Richard would think of Benedicta and if he would find her too clever to be attractive.

He knew that cleverness in a woman was tolerated only when they were old and could preside over a Salon of political and literary lions, such as Lady

Holland had achieved in the teeth of the antagonism of her contemporaries.

But a Salon was very much for grown-up men rather than boys, and the Duke wondered if, in his aim to prevent Richard from thinking of Delyth, he should have turned to play-actresses and doxies.

"Time will tell," he told himself.

Nevertheless, he had gone on thinking of the problem and found that in consequence it was hard to sleep.

However, when Benedicta appeared at luncheon-time, he decided that he had been needlessly anxious.

As she came into the Library where the Duke and Major Haverington were waiting for her, they saw at first glance that something sensational had taken place in that she was wearing a new gown.

It was very simple and had, the Duke saw with an experienced eye, been run up hastily by the maids in the house from one of the rolls of muslin bought by the last Duchess.

It was white, and sprigged with tiny flowers of pale pink and green.

Sprigged muslin had been the fashion at the beginning of the century and the Duke suspected that young women now were wearing something different, but it was certainly exceedingly becoming to Benedicta.

Very simple, with a high waist-line, it had small frills falling over her wrists and one round her neck, tied in the centre with a narrow velvet ribbon.

She looked very young and very fresh, almost like a musk-rose just coming into bloom, or perhaps one of the celandines which made a carpet of yellow under the trees in the woods.

There was an expression of shyness on her face, as if for the first time she was conscious of her own appearance.

Then as she curtseyed to the Duke it was as if she forgot herself, and she said impulsively:

"I have something exciting to tell Your Grace, and

Hawkins told me that I could be the bearer of good tidings."

"What is it?" the Duke asked.

"Mr. Wood regained consciousness about half-an-hour ago!"

"That is indeed good news!" the Duke exclaimed.

"Hawkins gave him something to drink and he went to sleep again, but I am sure he is now on the road to recovery."

"I am glad, I am really!" Major Haverington said. "I know you have been worried, Nolan."

"I have indeed," the Duke answered. "It would have been a disaster if anything had happened to Richard."

The Major knew that he was thinking of the inheritance of the title, and he smiled before he said to Benedicta:

"The Duke is very attached to his young cousin."

"I hope Your Grace will be able to persuade him in the future not to indulge in anything so non-sensical as duelling," Benedicta said. "I thought it was illegal."

"It is," the Duke replied, "but when it is a question of honour, nobody pays any attention to rules and regulations."

"Then they should!" Benedicta said. "Life is so precious that no-one should be so foolish as to waste it."

"I am afraid that after there has been a long war," the Duke said, "we are all inclined to think that life is easily expendable."

"I cannot bear to think of so many young men being killed or wounded," Benedicta said in a low voice. "When we were coming South, Papa and I found so many bereaved wives and mothers. Their unhappiness haunted me, and there was so little we could do to comfort them."

She spoke softly, and there was something so compassionate in her voice that the Duke thought it was exactly how a woman should feel about war.

Yet, he told himself, men would go on fighting.

When luncheon was over he said to Benedicta:

"There is a picture I want to show you in one of the Salons."

He glanced at the Major as he spoke, who understood he was not wanted and walked off alone towards the Library.

The Duke took Benedicta into a large and very comfortably furnished Salon which normally was used only when there was a large party.

On one of the walls there hung a picture of the Holy Family escaping into Egypt, by Cranach.

"I thought you would like this," the Duke said.

Benedicta looked at it and he saw a light come into her eyes.

It was a very beautiful and famous picture of the Flight into Egypt with the Holy Child surrounded by small, winged angels.

The colour, the expressions on their faces, and the radiance of the picture seemed to give it a light that many other pictures lacked.

"It is lovely, completely lovely!" Benedicta murmured as if she spoke to herself. "I shall always be glad that I have seen it."

"I thought it would please you," the Duke said.

"'Please' is a very inadequate word," she protested. "I am thrilled, ecstatic, enraptured! I feel as if it inspires me."

She made a little gesture with her hands.

"What a pity that everybody cannot see it. I feel it could mean so much more than a thousand sermons."

The Duke did not speak and after a moment she said:

"I know you are thinking that while this means so much to me, other people might not feel the same."

"How do you know that is what I was thinking?" the Duke asked.

"I can almost hear your thoughts," she answered, "and of course you are right. I sometimes think that Papa forgets that however eloquent he may be, there are always a great number of people who do not understand, whose ears do not hear what he says."

"We cannot live other people's lives for them," the Duke said.

"No, that is true," Benedicta agreed.

"But we can try to help them," the Duke continued, "and that is what I want to talk to you about, Benedicta."

It was the first time he had used her Christian name, but she did not seem to notice, and after a moment, when he knew she was listening to him, he continued:

"Now that Richard is conscious, I want you to help him."

Benedicta looked at him in surprise.

"How?"

The Duke chose his words with care.

"He has been through a rather difficult time," he said. "To be frank with you, he has been enamoured of somebody who is totally unworthy of him; a woman whom your father, I am quite certain, would denounce as being wicked."

"So that was why he fought a duel," Benedicta murmured.

"Yes," the Duke replied, "and now, as we believe he will live, we have to heal not only his body but his mind."

"And his heart?" Benedicta questioned.

"I think perhaps that is the most damaged of the three," the Duke agreed.

"How can . . . I help him?" Benedicta enquired.

There was a faint smile on the Duke's lips as he replied:

"I do not think many women would ask that question, and you especially would not, if you have ever looked in your mirror."

She looked at him in such a startled manner that he knew the idea of using her attractions had never crossed her mind.

The colour rose faintly in her cheeks as she said:

"I do not . . . think I . . . understand."

"Let me put it very plainly," the Duke said. "I

want you to amuse Richard, to entertain him and to
do everything in your power to make him forget the
woman with whom, quite misguidedly, he thought
himself in love."

Again Benedicta looked at him in a startled
fashion. Then she turned her face away to stare up
at the picture by Cranach.

"Men are like children," the Duke said quietly.
"They run after something that attracts them, just
because it is bright and sparkling, only to find when
they have captured it that it is garish and tawdry and
not worth the effort."

"That is . . . your opinion of what has . . . happened," Benedicta said, "but will Mr. Wood think
the . . . same?"

The Duke was surprised that she should ask
such an intelligent and perceptive question and he
knew that it went straight to the crux of the whole
future he was planning for Richard.

Aloud he said:

"That will be up to you."

Benedicta hesitated a moment, then she said:

"I cannot believe that anyone . . . in love . . .
really in love, could . . . change so quickly or . . . forget."

"Unless Richard is very much more stupid than
I believe him to be," the Duke replied harshly, "he
will realise that his love was just a mirage, and the
object of it too despicable and unworthy for him to
risk anything, let alone his life and health, on her
behalf."

"Are you . . . sure of this?" Benedicta asked.

"Quite sure!" the Duke said positively.

"He must have . . . loved her very . . . very much,"
Benedicta said.

The Duke's lips tightened.

He knew that Benedicta was thinking of what
had happened as something romantic and an expression of true love.

He could hardly explain to her that it was something very different, sordid and unpleasant, the betrayal by a faithless, lustful woman of everything that was decent and sacred.

He did not speak, however, and after a moment Benedicta turned from her contemplation of the picture.

"I will try to ... help him," she said, "because you have been so kind and because I owe you a ... debt of gratitude that can never be ... repaid. But if I fail ... you will not be ... angry with me?"

It was not what the Duke had expected her to say, and he smiled as he replied:

"I promise you that nothing that happens in the future will be your fault, and I shall be only too grateful that you attempted to help Richard."

"Then I will do my best."

They walked towards the door, then she asked the question which was, the Duke thought, the inevitable feminine one:

"Was she very ... beautiful?"

"Very!" he answered. "But I am sure you will find her counterpart in the Bible in Jezebel."

"She was eaten by the dogs."

That, the Duke told himself savagely, was exactly what he hoped would happen to Delyth, although it was unlikely.

Aloud he said:

"I daresay we shall find that some other unpleasant punishments await those who are wicked. It is a long time since I have read my Bible carefully."

"Papa's punishments for sinners used to haunt me when I was a child," Benedicta replied. "Mama always comforted me by saying that she never for a moment believed they were half so cruel as they sounded."

"Well, one thing of which we can be quite certain," the Duke said bitterly, "is that Richard has been punished."

They had reached the Hall and he knew that Benedicta intended to go upstairs to her father.

"Shall we go and see our invalids together?" he asked.

"Please let us do that," she answered.

They climbed the carved staircase side by side and walked along the passage which led to Richard's room in the South Wing.

The sunshine was coming through three windows which overlooked the garden, and the heir to Kingswood lay in a big four-poster bed draped with embroidered curtains.

He was covered with a bed-spread which had also been embroidered centuries earlier by loving hands.

As they entered the room, the young footman whom the Duke knew must be Jackson rose to his feet.

He did not speak, and the Duke and Benedicta walked towards the bed.

Richard was lying on his back with his eyes closed and the Duke thought that although his face was very pale, there was a sharpness about his features which was not usually there.

He looked handsome in a manner which should appeal to any young girl.

The collar of his night-shirt was very white against his chin, and his hair, swept back from his forehead, had a romantic look reminiscent of Lord Byron, who had started a poetical cult amongst the younger Bucks.

They stood for some moments in silence, then Benedicta put out her hand and laid it on Richard's forehead.

"He has no fever," she said in a low voice. "That is good. But he might have one later when he regains consciousness."

Her hand was very light but it awoke the sleeping young man and his eyes opened slowly.

Watching, the Duke thought he had a little difficulty in focussing them; then he saw Benedicta and there was a faint expression of surprise in his eyes.

"Where—am—I? What—has—happened?" he asked.

The words were slurred and hardly audible, and yet it was possible to understand them.

"You are quite safe," Benedicta said softly. "Go back to sleep."

He looked at her for a few seconds, then obediently shut his eyes.

Without speaking, Benedicta moved out of the room and the Duke followed her.

"I know Hawkins was afraid that your cousin might die," she said, "but he will live, although it may be a long time before he is well enough to do all the things he did before."

"That he is alive is all that matters."

She looked as if she would like to argue with the Duke, but she said nothing and after a moment he said:

"Of course I want him to be fully recovered, to be able to ride and do all the things he was doing before he was brought to this deplorable state."

"He will be all right," Benedicta said confidently.

"How do you know?"

She did not speak for a moment and he thought she would not reply, but then she said:

"I suppose it is because I have been with so many ... sick people, but I ... *do* know."

She thought the Duke seemed interested and she went on:

"There was a woman, two days ago, who asked Papa to pray for her. She was not very old, and she did not think she was dying, and yet I knew."

"What did you know?" the Duke asked.

"That she only had a little time to ... live. It was as if I could feel her ... slipping away, losing her ... hold on the ... earth."

The Duke looked at Benedicta in perplexity.

"I do not understand."

"Nor do I," she answered, "but I am convinced in my mind that what I feel is right, and that is why I am quite sure that Mr. Wood will get well."

They had reached the top of the staircase and the Duke asked:

"And what do you feel about your father?"

He saw a look of fear come into her grey eyes before she said:

"It is more . . . difficult to think . . . impartially when it concerns . . . somebody you . . . love."

"Let me come and see your father," the Duke suggested.

"I would like you to do that," Benedicta replied.

They climbed up to the next floor.

Benedicta opened the door of a room which the Duke knew was considered one of the secondary bed-rooms in the house.

It was comfortable and well appointed but could not compare with those occupied by Richard and by the more important guests who came to Kingswood.

There was no-one in attendance in the room and it was in fact unnecessary.

The man lying on the bed was quiet, but in a different way from Richard.

There was something immobile about him, and the Duke thought as he approached the bed that he would not be surprised to learn that the Reverend Aaron Calvine was already dead.

Perhaps Benedicta had the same thought, for, as she had done to Richard, she put her hand on her father's forehead.

She was obviously satisfied with what she found, and very tenderly she smoothed back his white hair and quite unnecessarily tidied the sheet in front of him.

"The Doctor saw him this morning?" the Duke asked. "What did he say?"

"He said there was no change and it was too soon to expect one."

She gave a little sigh, then in a lowered voice she went on:

"It seems so unlike Papa to be so quiet. He has always been so vividly alive."

"I am sure you are praying that he will get well," the Duke said.

"I have prayed and prayed," Benedicta replied.

"But then I . . . wonder if he would not be . . . happier if he was with my . . . mother."

Tears came into her eyes as she spoke, and to hide them she turned towards the door and opened it.

"I am sure Your Grace has a great many things to do. Thank you for coming to see Papa."

"There is no point in your staying here," the Duke said, "and I know that Hawkins will let you know the minute there is any change."

"Then what do you want me to do?" Benedicta asked.

"I am going to take you driving round the estate," he answered. "There is quite a lot I want to show you now, because I have a feeling that once our invalids are better, they will occupy most of your time."

He saw the excitement in Benedicta's eyes.

"May I really do that?" she asked.

"There is nothing to stop you," the Duke replied. "I suggest you get something to put round your shoulders, for it can be cold if we go fast."

She went into her own room without a further word and the Duke knew that she was thrilled by the idea of the drive.

He thought how easy it was to give so much pleasure to someone who was so unspoilt and unsophisticated.

Then it crossed his mind that almost any woman of his acquaintance would, if he extended his invitation, be delighted to go driving with him.

But he knew that as far as Benedicta was concerned, her feelings about him were very different from what theirs would have been.

He walked slowly down the stairs, and before he was halfway down the second flight which led to the Hall, Benedicta came running behind him.

She had a shawl over her arm which the Duke thought must have been provided by Mrs. Newall, but there was no bonnet on her head, and as he looked at her she asked:

"Will you be very ashamed of me if I come like

THE DUKE AND THE PREACHER'S DAUGHTER

this? I am afraid I left my only bonnet behind in the barn, and I do not wish to keep you waiting by asking Mrs. Newall if she has anything I could wear."

"You look perfectly all right as you are," the Duke replied, resisting an impulse to tell her that she looked indeed very lovely.

He thought that she would not understand and would perhaps question any compliment he might pay her.

"Then that is all right," Benedicta said, as a child might have done. "I cannot tell you how I have longed to drive behind some really well-bred horses. I used to feel so envious when they passed us on the road."

"While you are at Kingswood there is no need for you only to drive. You can ride?"

Benedicta's eyes were like stars.

"Could I do that?" she asked. Then her eyes fell as she added, "But I have no riding-habit."

"I am sure Mrs. Newall will be able to find you one," the Duke said casually, making a note that one must be procured, whatever the difficulties it might entail.

"I do hope she has," Benedicta said. "She told me she had lots of things which nobody wanted and which would have been thrown away except that she is what she calls the 'hoarding sort.'"

"It has certainly turned out to be a useful habit," the Duke said with a smile, "and of course there is plenty of room in this house for a great number of things to be hoarded."

"It is the largest house I have ever been in," Benedicta said, "and quite the most beautiful!"

"I am glad it meets with your approval," the Duke said slightly sarcastically.

"Mama used to tell me about the houses she visited when she was a girl, and though they sounded very grand, they could not have been as magnificent as Kingswood."

The Duke thought that was true, but he was engaged with ordering his Phaeton to be brought to the front door immediately and therefore made no reply.

Leaving Benedicta in the Hall, he walked into the Library.

The Major was sprawling in an arm-chair, ostensibly reading the newspaper but actually half-asleep.

"Where have you been, Nolan?" he enquired drowsily.

"Inspecting the invalids," the Duke said. "Richard has regained consciousness and is definitely better."

"Thank God for that!" the Major replied. "What do you want to do?"

"I am taking Benedicta for a drive in the Phaeton," the Duke answered, "but, as you know, there is only room for two."

The Major raised his eye-brows.

"I have already instructed her in what I want her to do as regards Richard," the Duke went on, "and she has agreed to try to divert his mind from Delyth."

"You did not tell her about Delyth?"

"Indirectly."

"Well, I suppose she should know what she is up against," the Major remarked, "although I should imagine that she has never come across anybody in that particular category."

"I should hope not!" the Duke said sharply. "Well, look after yourself, Bevil. We shall not be long."

"I am quite comfortable," the Major answered. "Be careful, Nolan!"

"Careful about what?" the Duke enquired as he walked towards the door.

"If Benedicta falls in love with you, your planned campaign will be sadly disorganised."

"There is no fear of that," the Duke replied. "I think she regards us both as being older than Methuselah!"

He left the Library as he spoke, and the Major lay back in the chair, an amused expression on his face.

He had a feeling that the Duke was playing a

dangerous game, and yet to watch it was undoubtedly
intriguing.

It was so like him, the Major thought, to be
apparently oblivious of the fact that his attraction as a
heart-breaker would make it difficult for a young,
unsophisticated Preacher's daughter to be interested
in another man, especially one who, at the moment
at any rate, was definitely out of the running.

He thought over the position for some moments,
then he closed his eyes.

'It might do Nolan good,' he thought to himself,
'but God help that child! She will be playing with
fire!'

*   *   *

If the Duke had been surprised at Benedicta's
appearance at luncheon, he was still more so when it
was time for dinner.

This evening they met in the Blue Salon, a room
decorated with French pictures which he thought
would interest Benedicta.

The walls were panelled with blue brocade and
picked out with gold, and the Fragonard over the
mantelpiece echoed the colours both of the ceiling
and the Aubusson carpet.

When Benedicta came into the room, it might
have been chosen as a background for her by some
experienced stage-producer.

She stood for a moment in the doorway and both
the Duke and Major Haverington saw that she was
wearing an evening-gown cut low at the neck so that
it revealed her white skin and having tiny puffed
sleeves which left her arms bare.

She paused, and in any other woman it might
have been a theatrical gesture to show herself off, but
the Duke realised that it was because she was shy.
Then she ran towards him.

"Tell me ... please tell me ... Your Grace," she
begged in a breathless little voice, "if you think this
gown is all right and not too ... revealing."

"Revealing?" he questioned.

"It seems so . . . low at the . . . neck," Benedicta said, "but Mrs. Newall was insistent that this is how I should . . . dress at my . . . age."

The Duke realised that she was seriously worried in case her gown could be thought "fast" or in any way reprehensible.

It was in fact a very modest, very simple garment, and it framed Benedicta's unusual loveliness. At the same time, it did not disguise the slender beauty of her figure or the grace of her movements.

"I think it is charming!" the Duke said. "And it is just how I should like my niece, if I had one, to be dressed."

He spoke deliberately, because of the Major's warning, which was still ringing in his ears.

He turned to his friend now and asked:

"Do you not agree with me, Bevil? I was thinking that your niece Jane is about the same age."

"She is," the Major replied, "but not nearly so attractive, might I add!"

Benedicta gave him a little smile. Then her eyes were turned towards the Duke and it was obviously his opinion she valued.

"You are . . . quite sure?" she asked.

"Quite sure!" he replied. "And may I say that I commend Mrs. Newall's taste and the manner in which she has produced such a delightful gown in so short a time."

"The housemaids have been working on it all the afternoon," Benedicta said, "and in fact it is not quite finished, but I did so want you to see me looking different."

"You will grace the Dining-Room," the Duke approved lightly.

But the Major noted that at the compliment there was a gladness in Benedicta's eyes that was unmistakable.

As if the new gown affected them all, the conversation was gayer and more amusing than it had been at any other meal.

The Duke told them stories of the war which

contained no horrors but which made Benedicta laugh as he had intended.

He described their exploits after the victory in France and made even the return of the troops to England and the difficulties of demobilisation seem quite amusing.

In return, Benedicta told them of some of the incidents that had happened on her journey down from Northumberland; she described how they had been chased away from houses by savage dogs, and how they had slept in places where ruffians had tried to pick their pockets and, finding nothing, had been dismally disappointed.

At a Fair, she had once, by mistake, won a suckling-pig and had no idea what she should do with it.

They laughed a lot, and when finally they left the Dining-Room to return to the Blue Salon, Benedicta exclaimed:

"I have never had such a wonderful party. In fact, never before have I dined with two gentlemen or known how exciting it could be!"

"We are flattered that you find us exciting," the Major said.

"Wait until Richard is well," the Duke interposed. "Then our noses will certainly be put out of joint!"

"That is untrue!" Benedicta objected quickly. "How could you think that I would rather be with anyone but you . . . both?"

She added the last word, but she was looking only at the Duke. The Major thought that the inevitable was happening and wondered what he could do about it.

Then before anyone else could speak, the door of the Salon opened and the Butler announced:

"Lady Delyth Maulden, Your Grace!"

Chapter Four

For a moment it seemed as if everyone in the Salon had turned to stone.

Only Lady Delyth was completely self-assured as she curtseyed to the Duke with a gesture that was somehow both mocking and ironic.

"I have brought Your Grace good news which I am sure you are anxious to hear."

The Duke did not speak, but Benedicta, watching, thought that she had never seen another woman who was so beautiful, so glittering, or so glamorous.

Lady Delyth was wearing a gown of emerald-green silk which, with its low décolletage and transparent over-skirt, made her appear as alluring and at the same time as dangerous as a snake.

There were emeralds round her long white neck and shining in her dark hair, and in Benedicta's eyes she looked as if she came from another world and was not human in the ordinary sense of the word.

Lady Delyth did not wait for the Duke to reply but continued:

"I knew you would be thrilled to hear, and you too, Major Haverington, that the Magistrates have decided that Sir Joceline's death was one of misadventure, so we need no longer be worried about poor Richard."

There was an unmistakable scowl between the Duke's eyes.

He was already aware of what Lady Delyth was

telling him, for he had sent not only an experienced
Lawyer but his Comptroller and Dr. Emerson to
the Court to be ready to represent Richard, should
the occasion arise.

With his usual efficiency, he had already seen
the High Sheriff and the Chief Magistrates and told
them that Richard was on the point of death and it
would be difficult to attribute the blame of what had
occurred to either of the gentlemen concerned.

As the Duke had tremendous influence in the
County, it was not surprising that the verdict was one
of exoneration, and all three men who had been present on his instructions had informed him of what had
occurred earlier in the day.

As Lady Delyth finished speaking, he merely
asked bluntly, in an uncompromising tone of voice
which showed that he was considerably incensed:

"May I enquire why you are here?"

"I should have thought that was obvious," Lady
Delyth replied.

As she spoke, she looked at him from under her
eye-lashes, appearing so seductive as she did so that
Benedicta could not take her eyes from her face.

"I have called to see my fiancé. I would have
done so before, but unfortunately I was rendered
prostrate with shock from the tragedy which occurred
the other night."

The Duke paused before replying, as if he was
choosing his words with care. Then he was aware of
the rapt manner in which Benedicta was looking at
Lady Delyth.

He said to her quietly:

"I think, Benedicta, that Hawkins will be waiting
to report to you on your father's condition before he
goes downstairs to his supper."

"Yes, of course."

Benedicta curtseyed.

"Thank you, Your Grace, for a most interesting
evening."

Moving past Lady Delyth without looking at her,
she left the room.

"Who was that?" the latter questioned curiously.

"Whom I entertain in my house does not concern you," the Duke replied. "You have come here uninvited, and now I ask you to leave."

Lady Delyth's eyes opened in affected surprise.

"Can you really be so impolite?" she asked. "I have called to see Richard, which I intend to do."

"I think you are under some misapprehension," the Duke replied. "To begin with, my cousin is not in a fit state to see anyone; and secondly, your behaviour the other evening has forfeited any claim you might have had on his affections."

"He has asked me to be his wife," Lady Delyth replied, "and I have accepted."

The Duke seemed to grow taller and more imposing. Then he said in a voice that had intimidated many of those who had misbehaved while serving under him.

"Your association with any member of my family is finished. You will neither see nor communicate with Richard again."

Lady Delyth smiled and it gave her face a somewhat sinister expression.

"My dear Duke, you are being very autocratic! Have you forgotten that one word from me and Richard will stand trial for murder?"

She paused to let her words sink in, then continued:

"The theatrical performance I gave on your instructions when the High Sheriff arrived the other evening was very convincing, and indeed without boasting I can say I am a most proficient actress."

Her eyes met the Duke's defiantly as she went on:

"But of course a fragile woman like myself, in such tragic circumstances, may easily on the spur of the moment tell a story which is not quite accurate and possibly may be mistaken concerning the sequence of events."

Her voice sharpened as she added:

"Richard will marry me, or I will retract my

statement which was read out in Court this morning."

Now the Duke's eyes hardened and there was an ironic twist to his lips as he exclaimed:

"Very dramatic, Lady Delyth! As you say, you should do well in a Playhouse, but unfortunately your knowledge of the Law does not match up to your spite, your avarice, or your desire for respectability."

"What do you mean by that?"

Lady Delyth lifted her chin defiantly and the Duke noticed that she cast a glance at Major Haverington, as if looking for some support just in case her position was not as strong as she fancied.

"What I mean," the Duke said slowly, "is that the Law of England is quite firm on one point: a man cannot be tried or, as in this case, charged twice for the same crime."

He saw that this was a surprise to Lady Delyth, and from the way the expression on her face altered, he knew that she was suddenly tense.

"Therefore," the Duke went on, "as you have just told me, Richard is a free man. Whatever you may say now, however much you may try to blackmail him or me, you will be unsuccessful."

He paused to let his words sink in; then with his voice as cutting as a whip, to the woman standing in front of him he added:

"There are also stringent punishments for blackmailers, such as public flogging, and even transportation for life! Remember, you have threatened me before a witness, and make no mistake, I shall not hesitate to bring you before the Justices."

"You would not dare!"

The words were low and seemed to come from her lips almost like a hiss.

"Anyone who knows me," the Duke said slowly, "will tell you I am no coward when it comes to taking the offensive against an enemy."

"I will call your bluff!" Lady Delyth threatened. "Either you accept the fact that I am to be Richard's wife, or I will go straight from here to the High Sheriff."

"You must do exactly as you please," the Duke answered, "but I am not speaking idly when I tell you that my charge of blackmail will be before the Magistrates tomorrow morning, and as the Assizes take place within a few weeks' time, they will undoubtedly send such a serious charge to the Old Bailey."

Lady Delyth was defeated and she knew it.

The calm, assured way in which the Duke spoke, his overwhelming presence, and her knowledge that it would be impossible, even if she wished to, to fight an expensive and protracted Court Case, swept away her confidence and she was left defenceless.

Woman-like, she tried another tactic.

"If you are talking in terms of the Law, Your Grace, I must protest!" she said. "You have not heard my side of the story, and even the most common criminal is allowed to state his own case."

"I should have thought it was rather late in the day for excuses," the Duke said sarcastically.

"But not to explain that I had no choice in what occurred before Richard entered my bed-room," Lady Delyth said softly. "Sir Joceline was a strong man. He overpowered me, and I was not strong enough to fight myself free."

The Duke laughed and it was not a pleasant sound.

"A jury of idiots, Lady Delyth, might believe you," he said mockingly, "but I am not impressed, nor would I believe such a tissue of lies if you had a hundred witnesses to support you."

He walked towards the door and opened it.

"There is really no more to be said, and I am sure Your Ladyship's conveyance is waiting outside."

For a moment Lady Delyth hesitated. Then as if she knew there was nothing she could do she moved slowly towards the door.

As she reached the Duke she looked up at him and said, with eyes narrowed almost to slits:

"God help me, but one day I will get even with you!"

The Duke did not answer.

He merely bowed ironically, and as Lady Delyth walked across the Hall to where the Butler was waiting to hand her into a carriage, he shut the Drawing-Room door.

*   *   *

"You have beaten me again!" Benedicta exclaimed. "Where did I go wrong?"

"You should have played your Knight," Richard replied.

His voice was still weak and his face very pale as he leant back against the pillows.

During the last ten days he had regained a lot of his strength and there was no doubt that he was improving.

At first when the fever had left him Benedicta had only visited him for a few minutes at a time. Then she had read him extracts from the sporting-pages of the newspapers, and when he could sit up she found that one game in which he was proficient was chess.

"My father used to make me play with him in the holidays from school," he had said. "I hated it then, but now I find it rather enjoyable."

"I have always loved it because it is such an ancient game," Benedicta had replied. "It fascinates me to think it was being played in India five thousand years ago, when in England our ancestors were walking about in woad, a very chilly fashion for the winter months!"

Richard had tried to laugh, but it hurt his chest and it turned into a cough, so Hawkins had come hurrying in, to shoo Benedicta from the room and make him lie flat.

"Do not make me laugh," Richard had extorted Benedicta after that. "If I cough, Hawkins punishes me as if I were a child. I am sick to death of looking at the canopy of this bed!"

But Benedicta did make him laugh, because of the things she said and because she was so unlike any other girl he had met before.

Now he remarked:

"I was thinking over what you said about chess coming from India, but my father always told me that the game came from Persia."

"I believe it was imported there under the Sanskrit name *Chaturanga*, in the sixth century," Benedicta replied, "but no-one seems to know when it first came to England."

She thought that Richard seemed interested, and she continued:

"There is, however, an interesting story that when King Canute was playing with the Earl of Ulf, they quarrelled so violently that the Earl upset the board and was in consequence murdered in Church a few days later, on the order of the King."

She was only trying to amuse Richard with the tale, but he went very pale and shut his eyes.

It suddenly struck her that the word "murder" had upset him, and she said quickly:

"You are tired. Let me read to you from a book I found in the Library; it is all about insects, and you may or may not be interested to know that to enable them to run fast, one species has twenty-two pairs of legs."

"Which undoubtedly was very useful for pickpockets," Richard remarked, and the laughter was back in his eyes.

The Duke and Major Haverington had gone back to London, and Benedicta thought that despite the beauty of Kingswood, she would have found it rather lonely if she had not had Richard to talk to.

Her father was still desperately ill.

They fed him nourishing soups, but he did not recognise anyone, and Benedicta sometimes felt despairingly that he had already died and left her alone.

At the same time, everything at Kingswood thrilled her.

When she was not in attendance on either of the two invalids, she would spend most of her time in the Library, sometimes not even reading but just touching the bound volumes with tender fingers, as if she caressed them.

Mrs. Newall had, by this time, supplied her with a quite varied wardrobe, with new gowns made, she said, from the rolls and rolls of unwanted material stored in the attic.

Benedicta also had a very elegant riding-habit that surprisingly had been cut out for one of the Duke's relations and then had been abandoned before it was finished.

Some alterations made it fit Benedicta to perfection, and when she rode either with the Duke or with a groom, she felt that she too was part of the magnificence of the house and the beauty of the gardens.

Every day these grew more lovely as the warm weather brought the trees and shrubs into bloom.

Pink and white blossoms on the peach and almond trees, hanging golden chains on the laburnums, purple lilac bushes, and the first buds of the crimson rhododendrons made Benedicta feel as if she were living in a fairy-land.

When the Duke returned from London he was told that she was in the garden, and as she ran towards him, against a background of colour, he thought her hair seemed part of the sunshine.

"You are back! You are back!" she exclaimed as a child might have done. "I am so glad!"

"You have missed me?" the Duke asked.

"The house has seemed very quiet without you, and yet sometimes in the Library I felt you were still here."

She spoke without thinking, then as she saw that the Duke looked surprised, a faint colour rose in her cheeks.

"I hope you do not think it ... presumptuous of me to have ... spent so much time in the ... Library?" she asked.

The Duke had thought she was embarrassed for a different reason, and he answered:

"I have told you that my books are only waiting for you to take an interest in them, and I hope in my absence you have, in every way, availed yourself of Kingswood's hospitality."

"I have ridden every morning," she said breathlessly, "and I hope you will think my riding has improved. It is such a long time since I have had a chance of riding a proper horse."

"What did you have instead?" he asked in an amused voice.

"A very old pony which could not move above a snail's pace, and sometimes when Papa was using him I had to make do with a donkey."

The Duke laughed.

"I can understand that my stable is more to your liking."

"Everything here is so wonderful that I sometimes feel I am dreaming."

"And Richard?" the Duke enquired.

"He is better ... very much better," Benedicta answered.

He thought there was a light in her eyes which he had not noticed before.

When he went to his cousin's room and heard Benedicta talking to him softly and intimately, as she might to a close friend, and saw Richard smile at almost everything she said, he told himself that his plan was working admirably.

Major Haverington had not returned to Kingswood with him.

In actual fact, the Duke had had a great deal to do in London, and his pile of invitations had increased day by day, but he had felt it imperative to return to Kingswood.

He was convinced that the reason was that he was still extremely worried about Richard.

Yet, that evening when he dined alone with Benedicta, he admitted that he found her more interesting than the ladies who had been waiting eagerly for his return to London.

"Tell me what you have been reading," he said.

Almost instantly they were thick in a conversation in which they disagreed with and contradicted each other, but he found that fundamentally they thought the same about the essentials of living.

As dinner finished, the Duke remembered what he had said to Bevil Haverington about warning Benedicta not to put Richard off by being too intellectual.

"Do you talk to my cousin like this?" he enquired.

Benedicta shook her head.

"Why not?"

"I do not think he would understand."

"Because he is ill?"

"Because he is very . . . young."

"So are you," the Duke pointed out.

"That is different."

"Why?"

"Because I have been so much with Papa and he is very clever and has an original way of looking at everything and everybody with whom he comes in contact."

"So you are merely echoing the thoughts he has put in your mind?"

Benedicta thought for a moment.

"I hope not," she said. "I believe Papa's genius is that he brings to the surface of people's minds what they were not even aware of within themselves."

She looked at the Duke as she spoke and added:

"I think that is what all great Leaders have done: they have not stuffed those who listen to them with new knowledge, but have made them . . . put into words or actions what was already in their minds, their hearts, and their souls."

"I had not thought of that before," the Duke remarked reflectively.

"I find that when I am with Papa," Benedicta went on, "he starts a train of thought, and then I develop it myself and it goes on growing until it becomes very important to me and part of my beliefs and convictions."

"We were talking about Richard," the Duke said.

"If I were speaking about him to Papa," Benedicta replied, "I would say, and he would understand, that Richard is a very young soul and he has a great deal to learn in this life and the lives that will come after it."

"You are speaking now of reincarnation?"

"How else can we believe in justice?"

"And I suppose you think you are paying in this life for the sins you committed in the past?"

Benedicta flashed him a smile.

"On the contrary," she said. "At this moment I am being rewarded for all the good things I did."

The Duke laughed, but it was only later that night, when he was in bed, that he thought of what Benedicta had said about Richard, and he wondered if the way she looked after him and the compassion with which she spoke was maternal rather than that of a woman with a man.

He gave a lot of thought as to what his next step should be.

He had no intention of allowing Richard to go back to London without first being certain that he would not be caught once again in the trap that Delyth Maulden had set for him.

Bevil Haverington and a great number of his other friends had told him that Lady Delyth was finding it hard to replace both Sir Joceline and Richard in her life.

The story of the duel, because it had caused the death of Sir Joceline, had shocked even the most hardened roués and dissolute lovers.

Not unnaturally, they guessed the reason why it had taken place, and as the Duke's cousin Richard had a social importance, it made them question Delyth Maulden's version of what had occurred.

For the first time in her triumphant progress as an acclaimed beauty, she was looked at askance by her admirers, and a number of the gentlemen who had fawned at her feet were a little more wary than they had been previously.

"Financially she is in a bad way too," Bevil Haverington told the Duke. "I believe Gadsby was very generous to her, and she is missing him on that account if not on any other."

"I hope she starves!" the Duke said vindictively.

"She will not do that, but I have a feeling she will still try to marry Richard, if only to spite you."

"Well, that is certainly something that must be circumvented," the Duke said.

Major Haverington, noticing the manner in which the Duke squared his chin and tightened his lips, knew that his friend would not take any chances where Delyth Maulden was concerned.

At the same time, it was difficult for the Duke to know how to approach either Richard or Benedicta.

He wished he was in a position to order them to marry each other as he could have done in the last century.

But he knew that however gentle and unsophisticated Benedicta might appear, she would not do anything that was against her inner instincts and perhaps her conscience.

They were looking at his pictures after dinner and he was showing her a very lovely picture of Venus painted by Boucher.

She was not in the least embarrassed that the Venus was completely nude, and he thought that that in itself was a strange attitude in so young a girl when she was looking at a painting and discussing it with a man.

"There are few women who are as attractive as that," the Duke said aloud.

"And if there were, where are the artists to paint them?" Benedicta asked.

"George Romney is now dead," the Duke said, "but he certainly created some very beautiful portraits of Emma Hamilton when she was young."

"I would love to see them," Benedicta said, "but perhaps I may never have the opportunity."

"Why not?" the Duke enquired.

She did not answer and he knew that she was thinking it was unlikely that she would be able to go to London, and there was also a question-mark over her future, which so far they had not discussed.

"You must ask Richard, when he is well enough," the Duke said, "to show you the other pictures in Kingswood House, which I know you would like."

"I do not think Richard is very interested in art."

"Then you must make him appreciate what is here," the Duke replied. "It will all be his one day."

"His?"

Benedicta looked surprised.

"Richard is my heir. When I am dead he will inherit the title, the house, and the estates."

"I was not aware of that."

"That is why it is extremely important whom Richard marries," the Duke went on.

"Of course . . . I understand."

Then she was quiet, and the Duke knew she was puzzling over something.

"What is worrying you?" he enquired.

"I was just thinking," Benedicta replied, "that if you married and had a son, then Richard would no longer be your heir."

"That is true," he replied. "But I have vowed never to marry, and Richard, I am quite certain, will make an admirable Duke."

"I wonder . . ." Benedicta said almost beneath her breath, but the Duke heard her.

"What do you wonder?" he enquired sharply.

"I do not think Richard wants to be a Duke."

"Why should you say that? What has he told you?"

"When he is well enough he wants to go to India."

The Duke was astonished.

"India! Why India?"

"He has told me that he has friends who are in the East India Company and he would like to live there for some years."

"It is an extraordinary idea," the Duke said, "and something I have never thought of in connection with Richard. But there is no reason at all why he should not do so, and later, when I am dead, become the Duke of Kingswood."

Benedicta did not answer.

When the Duke thought it over afterwards, he decided that it was a very sensible plan on Richard's part. He obviously did not wish to return to the London life that had proved so disastrous for him.

He was determined at the first opportunity to discuss with his cousin what Benedicta had told him, and the following morning he visited Richard early and found that he had passed a good night and had eaten some breakfast.

"You are getting better," he said cheerfully.

"Not as quickly as I would like," Richard replied gloomily. "It is damned dull, Cousin Nolan, having to be in bed all day."

"I am not going to say it is your own fault."

"But you are thinking it," Richard said accusingly, "and with good reason. I made a fool of myself, but it will not happen again."

"Benedicta tells me you would like to go to India."

"When I am on my feet I do not want to go back to London and have everybody laughing at me."

This was a different attitude from the one that Benedicta had intimated, and the Duke said:

"I think a trip to India would be most interesting, unless as an alternative you would like to marry and settle down. The Dower House is empty and it would be pleasant to have you on the estate."

"Marry?" Richard questioned.

"Why not?" the Duke asked. "There are plenty of very attractive young women of the right age— like Benedicta, for instance."

He saw as he spoke that the idea was one that had never entered Richard's head.

Wisely, he decided to say no more but to let the idea sink in. So, before his cousin could speak, he drew his watch from his waist-coat pocket and exclaimed:

"My horse will be waiting! I will see you later in the morning."

He went from the room and when he reached the Hall he found that Benedicta was waiting for him, in her blue riding-habit with a gauze veil floating from her high-crowned hat.

"I was just saying good-morning to Richard," he said, to excuse himself for being a few minutes late.

"He passed a good night," Benedicta said, "and Papa also slept peacefully."

"Then we can enjoy ourselves with a clear conscience, without worrying over our patients."

She smiled at him and a few minutes later they were riding side by side across the Park, the spotted deer scattering at their approach and the birds rising from the branches of the trees overhead.

The Duke glanced at Benedicta and saw that she was riding now with a grace and expertise that he might have expected was born in her. He noticed the lightness of her hands as they held the reins.

'She is lovely!' he thought. 'In fact it would be easy for any man to fall in love with her!'

Then an idea struck him which made him frown and he spurred his horse as if to get away from something which had startled him.

At luncheon they were joined by an elderly friend of the Duke's who had called unexpectedly to enquire about Richard.

But at supper they dined alone, and it seemed to Benedicta as if the table with its glittering gold ornaments and the Duke sitting at the head of it in his evening-clothes had an enchantment that was somehow different from what she had felt before.

She did not know why, but she felt as if everything had accelerated her mind into a new awareness.

The loveliness of the house, the presence of the Duke, the words they spoke to each other, the laughter which broke up the seriousness and the erudite trend of their conversation—all seemed to strike her afresh.

"I suspect that you are sharpening your brains with my books," the Duke said after they had argued

over one particular subject and she had eventually
proved to be right.

"I hope so," Benedicta replied. "There is plenty
of room for improvement."

"I can see that my house-parties in the future
will have to be composed of Oxford Dons who are
incredibly boring unless they are discoursing on their
own particular hobby-horse."

Benedicta laughed, then she said:

"While you were away I thought that perhaps
Papa and I being here was preventing you from
entertaining your friends as you would otherwise have
done."

"Why do you say that?"

"Even if they do not see Papa, it is rather depressing to know there is someone lying unconscious in
the house," Benedicta replied, "and I feel I ought to
suggest that we should go away."

"Go away?" the Duke asked. "And where do you
think you would go?"

She made a little gesture of helplessness.

"I do not know . . . perhaps you could . . . lend us
a cottage on the estate . . . just a tiny one, where I
could look after Papa and not be a nuisance to you."

"Do you really think that is what you are?" the
Duke asked. "And what about Richard?"

"I think Richard will soon be well enough for you
to invite some of his friends—his real friends—who
will talk about things they enjoy together, as I am
unable to do."

"Are you saying that you do not entertain Richard,
or that Richard does not entertain you?" the Duke
asked sharply.

"You sound angry," Benedicta said. "What I am
trying to say is that you have been so kind, so over-
whelmingly kind to me and Papa, but we do not
really fit into your life any more than I fit into
Richard's."

"Why not?"

"Because we live in different worlds. Richard

wants the friends he sees in London to come and give him the latest gossip about the mills, the wagers in the Clubs, the singers at Vauxhall, and those ... sort of things."

The Duke was silent and Benedicta went on:

"Please ... I do not want you to think that I am not ... completely happy here ... or that it has not been the most perfect thing that could ever have happened to me ... to be here at Kingswood, but I am only being honest in telling you that I cannot, now that he is getting well, supply Richard with exactly what he needs."

"I think what he needs is love," the Duke said. "Are you prepared to give him that, Benedicta?"

Her eyes were wide with sheer astonishment before she replied in a voice he could hardly recognise:

"What ... are you ... saying to me?"

"I am saying that it would make me very happy if you became Richard's wife!"

"Are ... are you serious? I never thought of ... such a thing. ... It never ... occurred to me."

"I know that," the Duke said quietly. "But I think it would not only solve Richard's problem but also yours, Benedicta. You need a home and a husband to look after you, and Richard would have much to offer you."

Benedicta did not speak, and the Duke, watching her face, knew that she was slowly assimilating what he had said.

Then at last she replied.

"Richard does not ... love me."

"Not for the moment, I agree, but it should be within your power, as it is with any woman, to make him love you and to make him happy. He would never have been anything but utterly miserable with someone as evil as Delyth Maulden."

There was silence for a moment, then Benedicta said:

"I think it will be a very long time before Richard

falls in love again. He may not have given his heart to the ... right person or to someone of whom you approve ... but love is never wasted ... never lost."

"What do you mean?" the Duke enquired.

"Love is not only something which we give to another person," Benedicta replied hesitatingly, "but it enlarges and enriches us, and, however much we suffer because of it, it adds to our ... spiritual development."

"You sound like your father," the Duke said scoffingly. "And you are speaking of a very different sort of love from what Richard felt for a woman who is utterly unscrupulous and without any principles."

"Richard gave her the best that he was ... capable of ... giving," Benedicta said firmly, "and that is what ... matters to him."

Again there was silence until Benedicta went on:

"I am sorry to ... disappoint you, and you know I would do ... anything in my power to ... please you, but I could not marry Richard even if he wished to marry me ... which he does not."

"Why could you not marry him?"

"Because I do not ... love him."

"You are obsessed with a lot of idiotic, romantic notions which are written about in books but which have nothing to do with real life," the Duke retorted.

"Perhaps not ... in your life," Benedicta replied, "but they have in ... mine."

"And in your life as the daughter of a travelling Preacher, who is likely to be worthy of this idealistic, spiritual love which to most people is only a lot of gibberish?"

As he spoke he saw her wince at his words. He knew that he had hurt her and felt glad that he had done so.

He had to shake her out of such ridiculous ideas and make her understand that what he was offering her was something that most young women in the highest social position would have jumped at with alacrity.

Because her obstinacy annoyed him, he said, his voice still sharp and commanding:

"Try to think sensibly, not with that unpredictable organ which women call their heart, but with your brain! You want money, you want security, you want a future in which you can produce children without wondering where their next meal will come from."

He watched her face as he went on:

"Make up your mind to attract Richard, and you will find that it is quite an easy thing to do. You will be benefitting him as well as yourself, and your future will be rosy."

There was silence, but his voice seemed to vibrate round the room and echo back at them.

Then after a few seconds the Duke asked:

"Well? What is your answer? You must have the intelligence to realise that I am talking sense."

Benedicta was staring sightlessly at the ornate gold vase in the centre of the table.

The Duke had the uncomfortable feeling that she was looking inwards at herself, examining her heart or her soul, and not, as he had asked her to do, thinking clearly and logically with her brain.

"Listen to me, Benedicta," he said. "What I am really offering you is Kingswood. Surely that means something? Surely you would not refuse, as no other woman is likely to do, to live here and be—a Duchess?"

Benedicta turned her face towards him. There was a look in her eyes which he did not understand, and her lips moved but for a moment no sound came from them, until at last she said:

"I am ... sorry ... desperately sorry ... but I could not marry ... anyone except the ... man I love."

As she spoke she rose from the table and without apology moved swiftly across the room and out through the door that led to the passage.

The Duke poured himself a glass of brandy and sipped it reflectively.

He told himself that he had done the right thing,

but he was not quite certain if he had done it in the right way.

He had surprised and startled Benedicta, but, because she was so innocent and so un-selfseeking, that was what he might have expected.

What he had not anticipated was that she would refuse him categorically.

He was certain that it was not because she had an aversion to Richard.

He had heard the way she spoke to him and he knew it would have been impossible for her to appear so sympathetic and understanding if she did not have some affection for him.

But that, the Duke was forced to admit, was very different from love.

He thought he should have realised that Benedicta, unlike most of the women whom he knew, had no social ambition and was activated by much higher principles and ideals than he had taken into his calculations.

Was it possible, he asked himself, that a girl without a penny to her name, and with a father on the verge of death, could refuse even to entertain the idea of being a Duchess?

He had never really contemplated for one instant that she would refuse the offer of such a dazzling future.

Then a thought struck him.

She had not said, "I could not marry unless I were in love," but, "I could not marry anyone except *the man I love.*"

The Duke knitted his brows together.

Had he really heard her aright? If so, had he, in making his plans, missed what should have been obvious—that Benedicta was already in love?

And if so, with whom?

The answer was not difficult to find.

Bevil Haverington had warned him from the very beginning that he himself might be the recipient of her affections, but she had certainly not made that clear, either by word or by deed.

Admittedly, she had looked pleased to see him when he returned home.

There was a kind of radiance about her when they rode or dined together, but that was not enough, the Duke told himself, for him to presume that it was due to him as a man.

The explanation could lie in the horse she rode, the environment in which they moved and ate, and the joy of being in the finest house in England, surrounded by treasures that would make any connoisseur gnash his teeth with envy.

There had been nothing in their association, he told himself, to make him aware, as other women had made him aware, that her heart beat any the faster because he was beside her.

With the women he pursued, or with those who pursued him, there had always been a kind of magnetism of which they both were tinglingly aware.

He admitted that it was basically a physical desire, an electric spark which, quickly aroused, could be as quickly extinguished.

Nevertheless, he had always been conscious of it, had always known that while the end was inevitable, there was much to be enjoyed before they parted.

But with Benedicta he had only talked, and their minds had been stimulated.

While he had enjoyed the intellectual challenge she gave him and at the same time appreciated her beauty, it had not entered his head that he should try to possess her, because he had been so sure that she was exactly what he required to settle Richard's life.

Now the Duke, who was usually so positive and determined and so completely confident of what he should do, felt strangely unsure.

"Dammit all!" he said aloud. "If she is in love with me, she has a strange way of showing it! Anyway, the sooner she realises that what she wants is impossible, the better!"

He drank his brandy and rose from the table in a bad temper.

'Women, always women!' he thought as he crossed the Dining-Room. 'They are tiresome, unreliable, and certainly unpredictable!'

He had never thought that Benedicta of all women would be like that.

Then he told himself even more angrily that it was what he might have expected, because she was different, so very different from any of the others.

Chapter Five

The Duke passed a sleepless night.

He found himself tossing and turning and was beset not only with thoughts of Benedicta and Richard but by another, more disturbing question which lay behind the whole problem.

Accordingly, he arose in an extremely bad mood and had a black look on his face, which, Hawkins knew of old, meant that he was fighting a battle within himself.

After having breakfast alone the Duke changed his mind about his plans for the day.

He sent away the horse that was waiting outside for his usual ride in the Park with Benedicta and instead ordered his Phaeton and went back upstairs to change his clothes.

He made no explanation to Hawkins as the valet helped him out of his highly polished riding-boots and into his skin-tight yellow pantaloons, which fastened under the insteps in the fashion set by the Prince Regent.

His superfine grey riding-coat, which had set a new fashion amongst the Corinthians, fitted him like a glove.

Finally, when his spotless white muslin cravat was tied to his liking, the Duke walked downstairs, a picture of fashion which was however belied by the darkness in his eyes and the hard set of his lips.

The Butler handed him his high hat, which he set

at a somewhat raffish angle on his head, and then he stepped outside to where his Phaeton was waiting.

In everything he did the Duke was a perfectionist, and the Phaeton which he had designed himself, with its black body and yellow wheels, was not only smarter but also considerably faster than any other vehicle of its kind to be seen in the London streets.

It was impossible to imagine that any man could look more impressive or more elegant as the Duke drove his Phaeton, drawn by four perfectly matched horses, away from the front of the house and over the stone bridge which spanned the lake.

Benedicta, who had been told that she was to ride alone, accompanied only by a groom, watched him from the other end of the Park as he passed along the drive.

She wondered where he was going and thought wistfully that she would have liked to be driving with him.

Then she remembered that the Duke was doubtless incensed with her, and she wished that she had not left him as abruptly as she had done last night.

She could have stayed even if it meant arguing and continuing to refuse to do what he wished, however difficult it might have been.

How, she asked herself almost passionately, could she agree to marry Richard, whatever the social advantages it might entail?

She was well aware that few women in her position would have refused to entertain such an offer.

Even her mother, who had hoped that she would marry into the Social World which she had known as a girl, would never have aspired to the pinnacle of her becoming a Duchess.

But that was not important, Benedicta told herself.

What mattered was love—the love that had made her mother insist on marrying an unimportant Parson, in defiance of her father's wishes.

It had been impossible for Benedicta, being so close to her father and so closely connected with many of the problems that were confided to him wherever he went, to be unaware that many men and women were desperately unhappy in their married lives.

It did not matter, she had often thought, whether they were rich or poor; when a man and woman were united by the bonds of matrimony, love or the lack of it could make their lives a Heaven or a Hell.

She wondered how she could make the Duke understand this, but she knew that in the Social World in which he moved, love was not important beside the advantages which a marriage could bring either to the man or to the woman.

Her mother had told her when she was a girl that her father, Squire Marlow, had tried to insist that she marry their neighbour, a nobleman whose estate marched with his.

"It would have been a brilliant marriage," Mrs. Calvine had said quietly, "and Lord Swinstead loved me in his own way, even though he was much older than I was."

She smiled before she added:

"But I had already given my heart to your father, and as far as I was concerned there was no other man but him in the whole world."

"That is the sort of marriage I want," Benedicta had told herself many times.

She knew even as she thought of it that what she actually longed for was impossible, a dream that had no chance of ever coming true.

* * *

The Duke drove extremely fast but with an expertise which ensured that he never took risks either with his horses or with himself.

It was a golden day, with the sun growing warmer and giving the countryside a fresh loveliness that had been proclaimed by poets since the beginning of time.

However, the Duke saw nothing but the road ahead.

The darkness was still in his eyes when after a

journey of over ten miles he turned through an elab-
orate gateway leading to an elm-bordered drive which
ended at an impressive red-brick house.

He drew up at the front door with a flourish, and
as liveried servants hurried down the steps he asked:

"Is Mrs. Sherwood at home?"

"I will enquire, Your Grace," the Butler replied,
recognising the Duke from previous visits.

The Duke, however, did not wait to hear if his
hostess would receive him. Being quite certain what
the answer would be, he stepped down from the
Phaeton and handed the reins to his groom.

He walked up the steps and into the Hall, and
as an attentive footman took his hat and gloves the
Butler came hurrying from the Salon.

"This way, Your Grace," he said, throwing open
the door.

At the end of the long, attractive room, with
windows opening onto the garden, a woman rose from
the chair in which she had been sitting with such
haste that the book she had been reading tumbled
from her lap onto the floor.

"Nolan!" she exclaimed before the Butler could
announce the Duke. "I cannot believe you are really
here! What a wonderful, incredible surprise!"

As the Butler shut the door of the room, she ran
towards the Duke, holding out both her hands, her
dark eyes sparkling with excitement.

"I thought you might be electioneering, Letty,"
the Duke said.

"George is doing that, and very disagreeable it
makes him!"

The Duke had anticipated that the Honourable
George Sherwood would in fact not be at home, as
he was fighting a by-election for the Parliamentary
Seat in the Constituency in which he lived.

"Let me look at you," Letty Sherwood said, holding the Duke's hands in hers.

Her red lips curved invitingly as she said:

"You have not changed, except perhaps you are

more magnificent, more handsome, and even more exciting than I remember."

"You flatter me!" the Duke said with a smile.

He released her hands and walked towards the grog-tray which stood in the corner of the room.

"May I help myself?" he asked.

"Of course," she replied. "Shall I ring for champagne?"

"Brandy will suit me," the Duke answered, picking up the decanter. "I am thirsty because I travelled here so fast."

"You wanted to see me?"

"That is why I have come."

"Nolan, I can hardly believe it! If you only knew how much I have missed you, and how boring everything has been since you left me for the nonsensical reason that you liked George too much to continue deceiving him."

She said the words lightly so that there was no reproach in them, but her eyes were very revealing as she watched him walk, a glass in his hand, towards the fireplace.

It was true; the Duke had used the excuse that he did not wish to deceive George Sherwood, as a way of ending what had been a delightful interlude with his delectable wife.

He had not been Letty Sherwood's first lover, nor was he likely to be her last.

But he had faced the fact that because she was becoming so passionately in love with him he was walking on dangerous ground, and an acute sense of self-preservation had made him extricate himself from the liaison before it went too far.

Today he had deliberately called on Letty Sherwood because he believed she would prove an effective antidote to a disturbance within his mind.

She was certainly extremely attractive, he thought now, and he had found her vivaciousness and her irrepressible *joie de vivre* hard to find in the women who had followed her in his affections.

Letty Sherwood was insatiable in her desire for what she called "love" and it was in fact the only thing she really enjoyed.

The Duke had often wondered, apart from the fact that she found him a very satisfying lover, how much she actually cared for him as a man.

There was no doubt that to have captured the Duke of Kingswood, if only for a brief period, had been a feather in her cap socially.

When they danced together or he sought her out at some Reception or Assembly, she seemed to sparkle almost as brilliantly as the diamonds round her neck, because she knew that every other woman in the room was envying her.

Now he told himself with a sense of satisfaction that Letty certainly cared for him enough to be undisguisedly pleased to see him again, even though when he had left her she had been genuinely distressed.

"You are here! You are actually here!" Letty was saying as if she could hardly believe it. "Why have you come?"

"To see you," the Duke answered.

"After not having come near me for almost a year?" she queried. "Really, Nolan, I am not entirely half-witted. There must be another reason."

"Perhaps I wish to reassure myself that you are as attractive as I remember," the Duke said slowly.

She smiled at him, but he saw that she did not believe him, and after a moment she said tentatively:

"Can it be Delyth Maulden who has brought you here?"

The Duke raised his eye-brows.

"What has Delyth Maulden to do with it?"

"That is what I want to know," Letty Sherwood answered. "The whole of London is talking about the duel in which Richard killed Joceline Gadsby."

"I am aware of that," the Duke said. "There has been no-one, from the Regent to the crossing-sweeper in St. James's Street, who has not questioned me about it."

Letty laughed.

"I am quite certain that that annoyed you. You have always hated questions, especially when you cannot answer them."

"Who says I cannot answer them?" the Duke enquired.

"Not really truthfully," Letty Sherwood said, "and do not bother to contradict me. I know there is something mysterious behind this whole episode, for if there was not, why should Delyth Maulden hate you so ferociously?"

"Does she hate me? If she does I am not aware of it," the Duke remarked.

"That, for one thing, is untrue," Letty Sherwood retorted. "But be careful. Delyth will do you an injury if it is possible."

The Duke took another sip of his brandy and Letty Sherwood said in a different tone of voice:

"I am serious! Delyth—and I have known her since we were children together—is a dangerous woman!"

"What are you suggesting she will do?" the Duke asked with a twist of his lips. "Shoot me? In which case she will hang for it."

"She might do something more subtle, like putting a snake in your bed or poisoning your food."

The Duke laughed.

"Those sort of things happen only in fiction," he said. "I think you will find that Delyth, like most women, just talks too much."

"Is it true that she is going to marry Richard?" Letty Sherwood asked.

The Duke shook his head.

"I can assure you, and this is the truth, Letty, that Delyth Maulden will not marry Richard, or, if she does, it will be over my dead body!"

"That is exactly what I am afraid of."

The Duke put down his glass.

"Stop trying to frighten me," he said. "Let us talk about ourselves. Why are you not at your husband's side soliciting votes? I hear he has a rather formidable opponent."

"Oh, George will win," Letty Sherwood said lightly. "And quite frankly I am sick of talking to yokels and kissing dirty babies."

"I should have thought there was quite a reasonable alternative to that at any rate," the Duke said.

For a moment two dark eyes stared at him questioningly. Then swiftly Letty rose from the chair in which she had been sitting and moved towards him.

"Nolan! Do you really mean that?"

Her arms were round his neck, pulling his head down to hers. Then her lips found the Duke's and she pressed herself against him.

There was something greedy and almost over-eager in Letty's kisses, which he remembered well. There was also the seductive, exotic perfume she always used, and the manner in which her body moved sensuously against his.

He had forgotten nothing, the Duke thought as his arms enveloped her.

Then he realised that something had changed, something was missing which had always been there before.

It was, quite frankly, that for the first time since he had known her, Letty aroused in him no response of any sort!

She was close to him, and he was kissing her, or rather she was kissing him, but the desire she had always ignited in him in the past and the flames of passion which had been an inseparable part of their relationship had gone.

For a moment the Duke could hardly believe it.

He had left Letty Sherwood when his mind had warned him to do so, but his body had still been easily aroused by her fascinating, seductive ways, with which she had attracted him in the first place.

Now, incredibly, he thought, he might have been kissing a stone.

Letty, however, was unaware of his feelings.

"This is like old times," she murmured against his lips, "and I want you! I want you as I always have done—and always will!"

She pressed herself even closer and kissed him again; then, still with her arms round his neck, she asked softly:

"How long can you stay? I take a rest after luncheon and George will not be back until tea-time."

It was an invitation which the Duke knew he dared not accept.

He had come to see Letty Sherwood because he believed that she was necessary to him at the moment and that the fiery desire which she had always been able to ignite in him would solve his immediate problem.

Now, incredibly, she had nothing to offer him, and he knew that somehow he had to extricate himself from this embarrassing situation.

"I am afraid, Letty," he said, "that while I would like to have luncheon with you, I shall have to leave immediately afterwards. I have an appointment which I cannot break."

"Oh—Nolan!"

Letty's tone was eloquent with reproach.

"I am sorry."

She kissed him passionately before she said:

"Never mind. It is wonderful to see you, and I shall be returning to London next week and we can meet there. It is really easier than here, as you know."

The Duke did know, and he stifled an impulse to say that he would be detained in the country all next week and would therefore not be in London.

Letty drew away from him but her mouth still seemed to be inviting his.

"I will just go and tell them that you will be here for luncheon," she said, "and also to make sure that George's best claret is brought up from the cellar. Then we will have a glass of champagne together, to celebrate your return."

She reached the door while she was still speaking,

and when he was alone the Duke turned round to look at himself in the mirror which stood over the mantelpiece.

As he tidied his cravat, which had been slightly crumpled by Letty's arms, he told himself that he was behaving like a cad.

But he really had had no idea when he had set out to visit an old flame that the fire which had still glowed amongst the ashes after their love-affair ended was now finally and completely extinguished.

"Why?" he asked himself. "Why?"

And he was afraid of the answer to his question.

Always he had remained friends with the women he had loved.

He did in fact occasionally return to them simply because some of the pleasure they had given him still remained alive.

Yet, where Letty was concerned, what he had felt for her was dead, completely and absolutely dead, in a manner which he had not expected.

She came back into the room and he turned almost guiltily from the contemplation of his own face.

With an experienced eye he watched her moving towards him over the carpet and appreciated the manner in which her fashionable gown moulded her figure and the way in which she carried her small head proudly upon her long neck.

He had always told her that she looked like a figure on a Greek vase, and as a connoisseur of beauty he had found that he enjoyed looking at her as well as touching her.

Now the former was still true, but he had no wish to touch her again.

Before she reached him, moving with the eagerness of a woman who knows that a lover's arms are waiting for her, he walked towards the window.

"Your garden looks better than I have ever seen it," he said. "Is that due to you or to George?"

"George!" Letty said briefly. "I am not interested in gardening, Nolan."

"But I am!" the Duke said firmly. "Come and

show me your lilacs, Letty. I want to order some more for Kingswood."

He took her hand in his and drew her through the French windows and onto the terrace outside.

"No, Nolan!" she protested, but the Duke was determined.

He thought to himself, as they walked side by side over the smooth green lawn, that he would still get his own way where Benedicta was concerned, but it was obvious that Letty would be of no help.

* * *

Because what he had planned had been a failure, and the Duke did not like failure, he drove back to Kingswood after luncheon in a rather worse frame of mind than when he had started out.

It had taken all his ingenuity to convince Letty that he could not stay with her and cancel the mythical appointment which was waiting for him at home.

Ostensibly she rested in her Boudoir, which opened out of her bed-room, and there had been occasions in the past, when her "rest" had provided them with at least an hour, when they would not be disturbed.

When he drove away the Duke knew somewhat guiltily that he had left behind a woman in whom he had aroused hopes which quite certainly would not materialise.

"What is the matter with me?" he asked himself savagely, and again he found it impossible to face the answer.

He drove home at a faster rate than he had travelled at in the morning, and there were even a few times during the journey when his groom looked at him in surprise, thinking that his master was taking unusual risks.

As they came down the long drive, Kingswood looked very beautiful enveloped by the afternoon sun.

But the Duke's eyes were still dark as he walked in through the front door.

"Mr. Jackson is waiting to see Your Grace, when

you can spare the time," the Butler said respect-
fully.

The Duke made no reply but merely climbed the
red-carpeted Grand Staircase and moved along the
corridor to Richard's room.

He rather suspected that Benedicta would be
there, and as he entered the room he heard her cry,
"Check-mate!" and add with an undeniable lilt of
excitement in her voice:

"I have won! For the very first time, I have won!
Admit it was clever of me!"

"Very clever!" Richard agreed ruefully. "I must
have been half-asleep not to notice where you had
placed your Bishop."

Benedicta clapped her hands.

"I wanted to beat you, and now I have suc-
ceeded!"

As she spoke, she realised that the Duke was
standing in the doorway and she rose to her feet.

Richard was not in bed but sitting in an arm-
chair in the window where the sunshine might bring
a touch of colour to his pale face.

It was only the second day he had been allowed
to get up and he was still very weak.

But the Duke knew it was only a question of
time before he would be back on his feet and able
to lead a more normal life.

"Hello, Cousin Nolan!" Richard exclaimed. "You
never came to see me this morning. I was told you had
gone driving."

"I had a call to make," the Duke said briefly.

There was something in his voice which made
Benedicta look at him a little apprehensively.

She thought she had never seen him look so
stern, or perhaps the right word was "imperious."

She had always wondered what he would be
like on a battle-field, and now she thought that this
was exactly how he would look, concentrated, determined, with an air of a man opposing gigantic odds,
and yet confident of being the victor.

She did not know why such an idea flashed through her mind, but it did, and quite suddenly she felt a little weak.

As if it was hard to stand, she sat down again in her chair, which was opposite Richard's in the window.

The Duke came and stood between them and Benedicta thought it seemed almost as if he towered menacingly over them, and her eyes were afraid as she looked up at him.

Richard, however, was unaware that the Duke's attitude was in the least unusual.

"I slept well, Cousin Nolan," he said conversationally, "and I know how much better I am. I will soon be riding again."

"The horses are waiting for you," the Duke replied. "But I think you are well enough to discuss your future."

"But of course!" Richard agreed. "I was going to talk to you about going to India as soon as I am well enough to travel."

"I offered you an alternative, if you remember."

"Of getting married?" Richard queried. "Well, I have no desire to do that, thank you, Cousin Nolan. I want to see a bit of the world before I settle down, although it was kind of you to offer me the Dower House."

He spoke in a slightly embarrassed way because Benedicta was sitting opposite him.

He did not suppose for a moment that the Duke had really been serious in suggesting that he should marry her. He thought it had just been a ruse to take his mind off Delyth Maulden.

"I have been thinking things over," the Duke said slowly, "and because you, Richard and Benedicta, are both so young, I have decided that I know what is best for you and therefore I will make the decisions concerning your futures."

Benedicta stiffened, while Richard asked petulantly:

"What do you mean?"

"I mean," the Duke said, looking at him, "that you certainly are not capable, as you have already shown, of behaving in a sensible manner or, for some years at any rate, directing your own life."

Richard gave a gasp and the Duke went on:

"I have therefore decided, as your Guardian, that we will have no further mistakes like the one that nearly cost you your life."

Richard was obviously stunned into silence, and the Duke turned to Benedicta.

"Last night, Benedicta," he said in an equally stern voice, "I made you a proposition. You refused it, and I have now decided that you too are too young and too foolish to know your own mind."

Like Richard, Benedicta could only gasp, and the Duke continued:

"I therefore intend to announce in the *Gazette* next week that you are betrothed and your marriage will take place as soon as Richard is strong enough. I do not intend to listen to any arguments on the subject. This is what will happen; but, in case you wish to defy me, I must point out two things."

The Duke looked at Richard again as he said, slowly and distinctly:

"You are dependent upon me for every penny you possess. I would not wish to threaten you, but may I say that you will find it very uncomfortable living without the very generous allowance you receive at the moment."

His face turned in the other direction.

"You too are dependent on me, Benedicta, for your father's accommodation and medical attention."

There was no need to say more.

He saw the colour leave her face and the stricken expression in her eyes.

For a moment there was silence. Then the Duke turned and walked from the room.

Neither Richard nor Benedicta spoke but only sat as if they had been struck by lightning and had no idea what to do about it.

Then with an effort Richard said:

"I have never known Cousin Nolan to behave like this. He cannot mean it!"

"He means it," Benedicta said quietly. "I am sorry . . . I should not have come here."

"If it had not been you there would have been somebody else he would have found for me," Richard said.

There was silence, then Benedicta asked:

"Do you still . . . love her very much?"

"Only in my mind."

He shut his eyes before he added:

"I know it is hopeless—impossible—I know exactly what she is, but I still want her!"

"I can understand that," Benedicta said, "and that is why you are right to go to India . . . to get away . . . because everything passes and gets better with time . . . even pain."

"That is what I hope will happen," Richard said, "for I cannot know she is so near and not try to find her."

"I . . . understand," Benedicta said again.

"You do not wish to marry me, do you?" he asked with sudden anxiety in his voice, as if he had not thought of her before.

She shook her head.

"No. I told the Duke last night when he suggested it that I would not marry you."

"You have no choice," Richard said, "although I do not believe Cousin Nolan would really turn your father out when you have nowhere to go and no money."

"I would like to believe that too," Benedicta answered, "but he is determined to have his own way, and you are dependent upon him. This is your whole life, although it is not mine."

"Then what are we to do?" Richard asked.

"I will think of something," Benedicta answered. "Do not worry but get well."

She rose as she spoke. Then she said:

"You are tired and this has been too much for

you. I will get Hawkins to help you back to bed."

"Thank you."

Richard leant back in the chair and shut his eyes. Then as Benedicta tidied up the chess-board he said:

"You are quite sure you do not want to marry me?"

She gave him a very sweet smile.

"Quite . . . quite sure."

"I have a feeling," Richard said tentatively, "although I may be wrong, that you are in love with Cousin Nolan!"

Benedicta was still and her eye-lashes were dark against her pale cheeks.

"You are!" he said in the voice of someone suddenly enlightened. "Of course you are! And it is not surprising. All the women fall in love with him, but he has sworn never to marry."

"Why?"

Richard shook his head.

"I do not know. Something happened when he was young. That is what my mother told me, and it made him determined that he would die a bachelor."

Benedicta's eyes were still on the chess-board, and after a moment Richard went on:

"I suppose if you really wanted to marry me we could make a go of it. You are awfully kind, Benedicta, and I like being with you."

"And I like being with you," Benedicta answered, "but you know as well as I do, that is not love. To be married and happy one must be in love."

"That is what I always thought," Richard said; "and I do not suppose I should have been really happy with Delyth. I was always so madly jealous of everything she said and did with other men."

He shut his eyes again.

"It would have been—better if I had—died as I—intended to do."

"You know you must not talk like that," Benedicta admonished. "Life is precious . . . a gift from God. It is a sin to throw it away stupidly and unnecessarily."

Her voice seemed to strengthen as she went on:

"I am quite certain that you will be a finer and better man because you have been through this difficult and hurtful experience. I am quite certain too that there are important things for you to do in this world, things you will not only enjoy but which will help other people."

Richard looked at her in surprise.

"Why do you say that?"

"Because I feel it is true. I can feel it inside me," Benedicta replied. "I am quite certain that in one way or another you will reach India, and it will give you what you are looking for."

"What am I looking for?" Richard asked.

"Only you can find the answer to that," Benedicta replied. "But you will find it, and what you have suffered will make you wiser and more understanding, which is what we all have to become eventually."

"You really think I will get to India?" he asked like a child being promised a treat.

"I am sure of it!" she said quietly.

She put her hand on his shoulder and he reached up and covered it with his own. For a moment they stood there and she knew that she both comforted and gave him hope.

Then she went from the room to find Hawkins.

* * *

The Duke, having keyed himself up to take a strong authoritative line with what he told himself were two reckless children, had been quite unreasonably put out when, as the Butler announced dinner, he was informed that Benedicta was dining upstairs.

He could understand that it might prove slightly awkward for her to dine with him. At the same time, he had looked forward to a battle between them, a battle which he was now certain he would win.

It was all very well, he told himself, to let young people think they had minds of their own, but when it came to fundamental issues, it was essential for someone older and wiser, like himself, to direct them to do what was right.

When they were older they would be grateful to him for saving them from themselves.

He was quite prepared to admit that it was partly his fault that Richard had got into such an impossible situation that he had killed a man and attempted to take his own life.

Now the Duke thought that he should have stopped Richard a long time ago, when he first began to associate with Delyth Maulden, from making a fool of himself.

He was quite prepared to admit that he had believed that a liaison with an older and very sophisticated woman might prove a useful part of his education.

But he had most unwisely overlooked the fact that Richard was young and impressionable enough to fall whole-heartedly in love with a professional siren.

He also had not anticipated, and for this he blamed himself, that Delyth would wish to become eventually the Duchess of Kingswood and that his own attitude towards marriage had, together with Richard's adoration, paved the way for her to seize the prize when it was offered.

"It was my fault—my fault from the beginning," the Duke told himself, "but now I have found exactly the right sort of wife for the boy. He will marry her and they will settle down under my eye, and we will have no more nonsense in the future!"

There was undoubtedly a warning at the back of his mind that it might not be as easy as he anticipated.

The difficulty, he knew, lay with Benedicta. However, she had to be provided for, and there was also another reason why he was anxious to dispose of her satisfactorily.

She might protest or try to pretend that she would not do as he told her, but after all, what woman could, when she thought it over, resist the enticement of being eventually a Duchess and mistress of Kingswood?

The Duke's lips twisted cynically as he thought how avidly he himself had been pursued for those very attributes, and how Delyth Maulden was still believing that through Richard they were within her grasp.

"I will announce the engagement next Monday," he told himself.

He had planned to spend the time at dinner telling Benedicta what sort of trousseau she would have and what special furniture from Kingswood could go to the Dower House.

She could do it up to her own taste.

'I will provide them with the right sort of servants,' the Duke thought, 'and of course they can use my horses.'

It was rather dampening, therefore, to find that his plans for the evening had been circumvented, and he sat down to dinner in an ill humour, sending away many of the dishes which the Chef had prepared so carefully.

"Tomorrow I will give a dinner-party," he told himself as the Butler left him alone with his port.

He decided he would also instruct his secretary to order the best dressmakers in London to send their representatives to Kingswood to plan Benedicta's trousseau.

She would certainly make a beautiful bride.

He found himself thinking of how she would look in her wedding-gown, with a veil which traditionally her husband should raise when the ceremony was over—to kiss her lips . . .

The Duke rose suddenly from the Dining-Room table, upsetting his half-empty glass of port as he did so.

Abruptly he walked across the room and along the corridor which led to the Library.

"What the hell am I doing?" he asked himself as he entered the room.

A fire was burning in the grate, and candles illuminated the volumes which covered the walls and which contained, he had often thought as a boy, all the information in the world.

Now it struck him that the books would reveal nothing to him, nothing that would help him at this moment.

He flung himself down onto a chair and stared into the fire, and his thoughts were not easy. . . .

* * *

It was nearly one o'clock when finally the Duke rose to go to bed.

He would have continued to sit there except that he remembered that Hawkins would be waiting for him and he did not wish to keep the little man up too late as he had so much to do during the day.

Slowly he walked from the Library into the Great Hall, and two night-footmen on duty sprang to attention as he appeared and watched him as he climbed the staircase to the first floor.

He had just reached it when he heard the sound of footsteps coming quickly down the secondary staircase.

The Duke turned his head in surprise and saw Jackson, the footman who had been nursing Benedicta's father, come down the steps two at a time.

He started to run along the corridor before he saw the Duke, and then he pulled himself abruptly to a standstill.

"What is it, Jackson? What has happened?" the Duke asked sharply.

"I was a-going to fetch Mr. Hawkins, Your Grace. I thinks the Reverend gentleman has passed away!"

"You will find Hawkins in my bed-room," the Duke said, and turned and walked up the stairs to the second floor.

The door of the bed-room of the Reverend Aaron Calvine was open and the Duke saw that inside it was lit by only one candle and the flames from the fire.

There was enough light, however, for him to see Benedicta standing by the side of the bed.

She must, he thought, have just come from her own room, which was adjoining.

She was dressed only in her white nightgown, her hair falling over her shoulders, and she stood very still, her hands clasped, staring down at her father.

As the Duke joined her he looked down at the bed to see that the Reverend Aaron Calvine was in fact dead.

He had not passed away in a coma, as might have been expected, but must have awakened for a brief period, as his eyes and his mouth were open.

As the Duke looked at the dead man, Benedicta turned and, with a movement like a child who seeks comfort, hid her face against his shoulder.

The Duke's arms went round her and he felt her trembling against him.

"Your father is dead," he said quietly, "but perhaps it is for the best. He could not have gone on as he was."

Benedicta did not reply and he knew that she was crying, but gently and softly, the tears running down her cheeks.

Holding her against him, the Duke was aware of how slender she was and somehow insubstantial, and he felt as if he held a waif rather than a woman in his arms.

Her head, which was only an inch or so away from his lips, smelt of violets, and he thought as she cried against him how young, vulnerable, and helpless she was, and how desperately in need of protection.

"Go back to your bed-room, Benedicta," the Duke said gently. "Hawkins will lay out your father and I will have him carried to the Chapel. When he is resting there, you shall see him again and know that he is at peace."

Benedicta did not speak and the Duke knew without words that she wanted to obey him but somehow was unable to move.

His arms tightened about her for an instant, then

he bent, picked her up, and carried her from the room into her own next door.

Here there was only the light from the fire to show him the way to the bed.

He laid her down against the pillows, then pulled over her the sheets and blankets, which she had flung back.

Now in the light from the flames he could see her white face and the tears glistening as they ran down her cheeks.

"I know you are sad," the Duke said, "but you said once that your father might be happier with your mother, and that is where he is now."

"I . . . know," Benedicta said in a voice that broke, "he will be . . . happy . . . but I shall . . . miss him."

On the last words her eyes overflowed with tears, and the Duke sat down on the bed, took his handkerchief from the pocket of his evening-coat, and wiped her cheeks.

"Try to sleep a little," he said, "and tomorrow when you see your father you will know that he is at peace."

He rose and, going back into the adjoining bedroom, shut the door behind him.

Hawkins was already there and the Duke gave him the necessary instructions.

"I'm sorry Miss Benedicta should have seen him like this, Your Grace," Hawkins said, looking down at the dead man. "I always thought he'd die without regaining consciousness."

"It must have been for only a second or two," the Duke said.

"Jackson said he only heard him make one murmur, Your Grace, and when he went in to him, the Reverend gentleman had gone."

"That is what must have happened," the Duke agreed, "but I do not wish Miss Benedicta to be upset."

"No, Your Grace, and Jackson and I'll get him down to the Chapel as soon as possible."

"I know I can rely on you, Hawkins," the Duke said.

When he reached his own room, he undressed himself and got into bed, and yet when the lights were extinguished he knew it would be impossible for him to sleep.

He could think only of Benedicta crying alone upstairs, and he knew that he wanted to comfort and protect her.

"How can that child face the world alone?" he asked himself.

He could still smell the violets in her hair and feel the soft warmth of her slender body.

Chapter Six

"*For as much as it hath pleased Almighty God in His great mercy to take unto Himself the soul of our dear brother here departed: we therefore commit his body to the ground, earth to earth, ashes to ashes, dust to dust...*"

The old Vicar intoned the words, and the Duke, who had heard them many times before, wondered if they sounded gloomy and depressing to Benedicta.

She was standing on the other side of the grave, her head bowed, the black gown which Mrs. Newall had hurriedly made for her accentuating the white translucence of her skin.

She looked very ethereal and more waif-like than usual, and the Duke longed to put his arms round her as he had the night her father had died.

He had found it impossible to speak to her the last two days before the Funeral took place.

He knew that she had spent every hour of the day in prayer beside her father's body in the Chapel.

The Reverend Aaron Calvine may in his old age have been a travelling Preacher, but he had lain in state in the same grand manner as the previous Dukes of Kingswood.

In an open coffin banked with flowers, he had looked very distinguished, with four huge gold candlesticks to light him in the darkness, and the Duke had ordered that the Chapel itself should be decorated with flowers from the greenhouses.

He hoped that somehow the flowers would make the solemnity of death a little easier for Benedicta, but she had not spoken to him since the night that he had carried her to bed, and the only news he had had of her came from Mrs. Newall.

"How is Miss Benedicta?" he had asked his Housekeeper that very morning.

"Very brave, Your Grace, as one might expect," Mrs. Newall replied.

Then as if she felt she had to explain she went on:

"It's those with faith, Your Grace, like Miss Benedicta, who realise death is not the end, even though it's always a sad parting."

"Yes, I understand that," the Duke replied.

At the same time, he thought that it was a strange conversation for him to be having with his Housekeeper and that only Benedicta could have caused her to speak in such a manner.

"Is Miss Benedicta eating proper meals?" he asked.

Mrs. Newall shook her head.

"The Chef has tried to tempt her with many special dishes, Your Grace, but as I told her myself, she eats hardly enough to keep a mouse alive!"

"We must alter that," the Duke said firmly. "I hope when today is over we can persuade her to have her meals downstairs again."

As he spoke, he thought how much he had missed her and how he was looking forward to their dining together and riding in the mornings as they had before the Reverend Aaron's death.

At the same time, the Duke was honest enough to admit that the death of the Preacher would make things easier both for himself and for Benedicta.

She had been right in saying that the presence in the house of someone who was dying cast a shadow, and the Duke knew that he had in fact been acutely aware of the man on the second floor who lay unconscious in a coma.

It was strange how it had affected him. He

thought that as he had seen so many men dead or dying, one more would have made no difference.

But because the Reverend Aaron was connected with Benedicta, he had always been aware of him in the background and in everything she thought and did.

Now he told himself that it would be easy to make her understand how concerned he was for her future and how essential it was for her to consider him her Guardian and allow him to plan for her in the way he wished.

The Service came to an end, and as the Vicar murmured the last "Amen" Benedicta turned and walked away from the graveside.

She moved towards the house, and the Duke, repressing an impulse to follow her, waited to thank the Vicar for his services and to see that the grave was properly filled in.

There were no mourners to whom he must be affable, for the only people who had followed the coffin as it was carried from the Chapel to the private graveyard were Benedicta, himself, Hawkins, and Jackson.

The two valets had stood a little apart and therefore only Benedicta and the Duke were actually at the grave.

He thought she would wish to hide her tears and he hoped that when she reached her bed-room, where he supposed she was going, Mrs. Newall would be there to minister to her.

The Duke offered the Vicar some refreshment, which he refused as he had another Service to take in the village.

Then the Duke was free to go back to the house and wonder how soon it would be possible to see Benedicta and to talk to her.

He went to the Library where the morning newspapers were waiting for him, but instead of picking them up he walked round the room restlessly, as if he could not settle.

He felt now as if for the last two days he had existed in a kind of No-Man's Land, having to force himself to wait impatiently before he could do what he wished to do or indeed take any action that was of any importance.

All the time his thoughts had been with Benedicta, and he knew that nothing else was of any consequence besides her and the future he was determined to arrange for her.

"Luncheon is served, Your Grace!"

The Butler's voice, from the door, startled the Duke.

He had not realised it was time for the meal and he knew that in fact he was not hungry.

Once again, as he walked towards the big Dining-Room he thought how irritating it was to eat alone.

"Miss Benedicta's luncheon has been sent upstairs?" he asked the Butler as he settled himself.

"Yes, Your Grace. The Chef has made a real effort, if I may say so, to tempt the young lady's appetite."

The Duke nodded, but he thought that like himself Benedicta would not be hungry.

'I must talk to her,' he thought to himself. 'It would be ridiculous for her to lapse into a depression and despondency because of her father's death.'

He thought that the sooner she discarded the black garments she had worn at the Funeral, the better.

Not that they had not become her—he found himself remembering how white her skin had seemed, and he thought that if he had been able to see them, her eyes would have appeared larger and more arresting in her face than they had ever done before.

'I shall persuade her to dine with me tonight,' he decided, and sipped the excellent wine that was in his glass without really tasting it.

He wanted to send for Benedicta as soon as he had finished his meal, but then he thought that that would be tactless.

It would also be uncomfortable if she refused to come to him.

Instead, he forced himself to go to the stables, where he had a long talk with his Head-Groom about certain improvements he wished to make in his blood-stock.

He also agreed to several alterations to the buildings which were overdue because he had shelved them as being unnecessary.

All this took quite a long time and when he returned to the house it was nearly four o'clock.

He decided that he would visit Richard, thinking at the same time that Benedicta might be with him.

He walked up the stairs, and as he turned towards Richard's bed-room he heard someone behind him and found that it was Mrs. Newall.

"Your Grace!" she said breathlessly, as if she had been hurrying.

"What is it?" the Duke asked.

"This is for you, Your Grace," she said, handing him a note. "I found it in Miss Benedicta's bed-room."

"You found it?" the Duke repeated.

As he took the note from Mrs. Newall's hand he had a strange feeling that he did not wish to open it.

He was sure that it carried ill-tidings, which he had no wish to hear, but because the Housekeeper was waiting he knew that there was nothing else he could do.

He opened the thick white paper, which was engraved with his crest.

For a moment Benedicta's hand-writing seemed to swim before his eyes and it was hard to read what she had written.

Then he read:

Your Grace:
I can only thank you with all my heart for your kindness to my father. I can never be grateful enough that on his last days on earth you did everything that was possible for him, and his Funeral was something I shall never forget.
I can only express my gratitude to Your

*Grace by saying I shall always remember you in
my prayers.*

> *Yours respectfully,*
> *Benedicta Calvine*

After he had finished reading what Benedicta
had written, the Duke stood staring at the piece of
paper he held in his hand, as if it were hard for him
to realise exactly what it said.

Then as he knew Mrs. Newall was waiting he
asked:

"Where is Miss Benedicta?"

"She's gone, Your Grace. In fact I think she must
have left immediately after the Funeral."

"Why should you think that?" the Duke asked, and
his voice was so harsh that it seemed to echo back at
him.

"The luncheon-tray which was brought downstairs from her room was untouched, Your Grace."

"How could she have gone?" the Duke asked
angrily. "Surely someone must have seen her go?"

"That is what I asked myself, Your Grace," Mrs.
Newall replied, "but if she left by the side-door while
the staff were at luncheon, it's unlikely anyone would
have been about the passages."

The Duke knew that this was true.

The staff ate soon after noon, before luncheon
was served in the Dining-Room, and it was always
a time when the whole house seemed quiet and
deserted.

"Miss Benedicta must have ordered a carriage,"
he said at length.

"I think not, Your Grace. She took nothing with
her."

"What do you mean—she took nothing with her?"

Mrs. Newall seemed to pause for a moment before she answered:

"From all I can ascertain, Your Grace, she was
wearing the gown in which she came here. I wish now
I'd thrown it away, but she wouldn't let me."

"The gown in which she first came," the Duke repeated.

He remembered the threadbare grey gown in which Benedicta had first appeared and to which she had added a Quaker-like little white collar the first night that she had dined with him and Bevil Haverington.

"It is absurd! Ridiculous!" he exclaimed. "I cannot believe this has happened."

"I'm afraid it's the truth, Your Grace," Mrs. Newall said, "and the only thing Miss Benedicta has taken with her is a pair of new shoes. I destroyed the ones she came in as they'd holes in the soles and weren't fit for a scarecrow."

The Duke stood thinking. Then without a word to Mrs. Newall he turned and walked down the passage towards Richard's room.

He found Richard sitting in the window, reading the newspaper.

He looked up eagerly as the Duke entered, but the expression on his face changed and it was obvious that he had expected someone else.

"Hello, Cousin Nolan!" he said after a moment. "How did the Funeral go? I hoped Benedicta would come and tell me about it."

"Where is Benedicta?" the Duke asked abruptly.

"Where is she?" Richard questioned. "I have no idea. I thought she would be with you."

"She has left the house! Did she tell you about it?"

"Left?" Richard exclaimed in surprise.

Then there was an expression on his face that made the Duke ask:

"You knew she was going? She confided in you?"

"No, I had no idea she meant to leave; at least..."

"Tell me what you know. You are hiding something from me!" the Duke said accusingly.

"I am not," Richard replied, "but if she has gone, I know why."

"Why?"

The question was like a pistol-shot.

"Because you told her she had to marry me and she has no wish to do so."

"She could have discussed it with me without running away in this absurd manner," the Duke objected.

"Would you have listened?" Richard asked.

The Duke did not reply. Then after a moment he said:

"You had an idea she might leave. Did she tell you where she would go?"

"No. She did not tell me exactly what she intended to do," Richard replied. "She merely said she would think of something, and this is what she must have meant."

"I will fetch her back."

"What would be the point?" Richard asked. "She will not do what you ask, and besides, although I like Benedicta very much, I do not want to marry her."

The Duke said nothing and after a moment Richard added:

"You could hardly expect me to, considering that she is in love with you!"

There was a moment of silence, and the expression on the Duke's face made Richard draw in his breath. Then surprisingly the Duke said in a quiet and different tone of voice:

"What makes you think that?"

"It was obvious from the way she looked at you, and when I asked her—she did not deny it."

The Duke did not speak and after a moment Richard said bravely:

"I told her that you had sworn never to marry, but she understood—as you refuse to do—that neither of us could marry anyone unless we were in love."

"Are you sure Benedicta is in love with me?" the Duke asked, still in the quiet voice he had used before.

"It would be extraordinary if she were not!" Richard observed defiantly. "Most women seem ready to chuck their heart at your feet. But Benedicta is different, so I expect it means more to her than it does to the rest of them."

"Yes, Benedicta is different ..." the Duke agreed, and walked from the room.

* * *

It was four hours later when the Duke really began to worry.

He had thought at first that it would be quite easy for him to find Benedicta, for he was certain that she would go north.

He reckoned that if she had started out after the Funeral, as Mrs. Newall had suggested, she would still be on the Kingswood estate, unless she had been able to walk more quickly than he calculated she could.

He had the idea that unless she intended to take a Stage-Coach, which he was sure she could not afford, she would keep to the fields and off the main highways.

At the same time, as she drew nearer to London she would inevitably find her way intersected by lanes and roads, where the Duke knew she would be in danger.

There were beggars, footpads, cut-throats, and raffish characters of all sorts and descriptions, who would constitute a definite danger to a young girl as beautiful as Benedicta travelling by herself.

The Duke had ridden his horse at a tremendous speed for the first part of the afternoon.

Because he knew he had a wide area to traverse, he had zig-zagged his way backwards and forwards so as to cover every route leading northwards that Benedicta might have chosen.

There were not only pastures and fields sown with crops to traverse, there were woods and copses, barren land covered with shrubs, and even swamps that were the breeding-ground of snipe but little use for anything else.

It was one thing to ride over them, but the Duke

was aware that they were far more difficult for a traveller on foot.

He was sure that Benedicta would not be able to travel at all fast, yet he had crossed the brow of the last hill overlooking the northern border of his estate without a sign of her.

He was now passing through a small valley and he wondered where he could look next.

All afternoon, every minute that he was riding in search of Benedicta, the Duke had been facing the truth—that if he did not find her again, he would have lost everything that mattered to him in his life.

It had taken a long time for him to be honest and admit to himself that what he felt for Benedicta was not the consideration and affection of a Guardian but the love of a man for a woman.

He had been so positive for so many years that he would never love any woman enough to need her permanently in his life that he had fought every inch of the way against his own feelings, his own inclinations, and the cry of his own heart.

But now he knew that he could no longer go on pretending, and he had to face the fact that he was in love, wildly in love in a way that he could not deny.

He had tried ever since meeting Benedicta to go telling himself that he would never marry anyone, that no woman should bear his name, and that he would remain, as he had always averred, a bachelor to his dying day.

Now he admitted that he wanted Benedicta as a part of himself, as his wife and the mother of his children.

He had been two years younger than Richard was now when he had vowed that he would never marry and that no woman should, as his wife, make a fool of him or defame his name.

It was shock that had made him feel like that, and shock that had made him grow almost instantaneously from an idealistic, adolescent boy into a bitter, resentful man.

He could remember all too vividly the evening when he had come home unexpectedly from Oxford, thinking what a delightful surprise it would be for his parents.

He had as usual bought a present for his mother, for he never returned home without bringing her one, and he knew how her eyes would light up with pleasure when she saw what he carried.

She would raise her face to his for a kiss, and then in her lilting voice, which always made her seem just as young as he was, she would exclaim:

"How heavenly of you, Nolan darling, to think of me, and of course it is just what I wanted! How could you have been so clever!"

He had arrived home at nearly ten o'clock. His home in those days was a house in Hampshire where his father bred horses which never won a race but which gave him a great deal of pleasure.

The old Butler whom Nolan had known since childhood was obviously surprised when he saw who was at the door.

"Why have you come home, Master Nolan?" he enquired. "We weren't expecting you for another three days."

"Yes, I know, Bates," Nolan answered, "but I finished my exams and there was no point in my staying on with nothing to do. Where is Papa?"

"He's at Newmarket, Master Nolan, and won't be home till tomorrow."

"Oh, how disappointing! I wanted to surprise him," Nolan said. "And where is my mother?"

The old Butler obviously hesitated before he said:

"Now you go up to your room and tidy yourself up, Master Nolan, and I'll tell the mistress you're here."

"You will do nothing of the sort, Bates! I want to surprise her, and if you want something to do you can get me something to eat. I have been travelling for hours and I am extremely hungry."

He did not wait to hear the Butler's reply but

hurried up the stairs three at a time and ran along the corridor which led to his mother's bed-room.

She and his father occupied the Master Suite on the south side of the house.

There was a large bed-room, a dressing-room, and a Boudoir which Nolan had always thought ever since he was a child was the most beautiful room in the house.

It was where his mother kept her treasures, wrote her letters, and sewed, and it was also where she had read to Nolan, sitting next to him on the sofa, when he had been a child.

It was there that he could talk to her, tell her confidences, reveal his thoughts and feelings, and sometimes shyly read her the poems he wrote, which he would never have shown to anybody else.

He reached the door of the Boudoir and paused for a moment.

Then, assuring himself that the gift for his mother was safely tucked under his arm, he swept the dark hair back from his forehead so that he would appear as tidy and handsome as she liked him to look.

He opened the door quietly.

He thought that perhaps she would be sitting in front of the fire as she often did, sometimes wearing only a lace-trimmed négligée in which, he thought, with her hair falling over her shoulders, she looked like an angel.

He saw, by the light of a few candles that were lit in the room, that she was not there.

There was, however, the scent of roses and a fragrance of other flowers which he had always associated with his mother.

'She will be in bed,' Nolan thought to himself.

Then he thought with a smile that if she was asleep, he would awaken her with a kiss so that she would open her eyes in surprise to see him beside her.

He walked quietly across the room, but as he neared the communicating-door which led to the bed-room he heard voices.

'So Papa is back!' he thought in surprise. 'I wonder why Bates thought he was returning tomorrow.'

Then he heard his mother say:

"Oh, Bernard! I love you! You know I love you!"

"My darling, my sweet! There is no-one in the world as beautiful as you!" a man's voice replied. "If only I could keep you with me forever!"

Nolan had stood as if turned to stone.

He had known immediately who Bernard was. He had known too that the last time he had been at home he had been very blind and very childish not to realise what was happening.

But that his mother should do this was so unbelievable that he felt as if he had been stabbed in the heart.

He had worshipped her, not only for her beauty but for her mind and her understanding, and because she personified everything that was pure, perfect, and beyond reproach.

Every woman he had ever met or seen he compared to her, and always he found them wanting.

But now his mother was no better than the actresses about whom his undergraduate friends sniggered, or the prostitutes who solicited young men like himself, when he walked back at night to his College.

His mother! His mother!

He had turned quietly and left the Boudoir, and when he reached his own room he swore that he would never marry!

He would never be deceived by a woman, and would never believe in one again or in the love they talked about so glibly but which was only another name for lust.

He had never spoken to a soul of what he had discovered, and as soon as he left Oxford he went into a Regiment and was glad that it kept him away from his mother and father.

As he grew older, he found women amusing and indispensable.

But while he gave them his body, his heart remained untouched, and in his mind he despised them for their frailty, and for the manner in which they were all too eager to offer him their favours and be unfaithful to their husbands.

If he felt compassionate towards anyone, it was the husbands whom he, like so many other men, deceived.

He would often' think of his father and wonder if he ever had the slightest inkling that his wife was being unfaithful.

When his father died Nolan was certain that he had lived in a "Fool's Paradise," and he watched his mother's show of grief with a cynical twist of his lips and a hard expression in his eyes.

"A fine performance!" he told himself when she cried bitterly at his father's Funeral.

When she married again, two years later, it had been with difficulty that he restrained himself from telling the man she married, who was obviously infatuated with her, that he was an idiot to trust her.

There had been dozens of women in the Duke's life, in London, Portugal, and France, but they had never meant any more than a short respite from his other occupations.

"Women are like flowers," he had said once to Bevil Haverington. "Pick them and they soon die. It would be best for one just to admire them and pass on."

"Best for whom?" Bevil asked. "And how could one be so unadventurous?"

The Duke did not speak and the Major continued:

"To me a new woman is always an adventure. It is like exploring a strange country, with the hope that one will strike treasure. Always one is disappointed, but that is part of the game."

"Perhaps that is the right way of looking at it," the Duke agreed.

"I have a feeling," Bevil Haverington said, "that you are looking for the crock of gold at the end of the rainbow. Fairy-gold, Nolan, which vanishes when you touch it! So be content with what is not so elusive and out of reach."

"I am perfectly content as I am," the Duke said positively.

Now he knew that that was not true.

He wanted what he had never wanted before—a woman to belong to him, to possess, and not just for a night or a short period of time but for life.

He asked himself how he could have changed so quickly and so unexpectedly.

But he had known from the very moment he first saw Benedicta, with her big eyes looking up at him as she pleaded for help, that she was different in every way from any other woman he had met before.

He had talked to her and been stimulated by her mind, and they had duelled with each other in words.

Surprisingly, he had wanted to impress her and please her, and without his realising it she had crept beneath his defences until finally the last barrier had fallen.

Now that he had lost her, he knew that he must find her again, because she was his, every precious piece of her.

He had denied the truth to himself day after day, night after night, until she had turned to him for consolation because her father had died, and he had held her in his arms.

He had known then, as he felt her slim body trembling beneath her nightgown and when he lifted her in his arms, that everything that was idealistic in him had been reawakened.

His cynicism and his contempt for women had been stripped away as if by a magic wand.

Now he knew that love had made him as vulnerable as he had been as a boy and that the hard, harsh veneer which had encased him throughout the long years of war had vanished.

The Duke reined in his horse and looked across

the valley where the corn, still green, was standing high in the fields.

On the border of his estate he saw a farm which he had not visited recently but which he knew belonged to a tenant-farmer, an old Scotsman who had been there for many years and was a rather surly, dour man.

Beyond the farm was a thick wood, half of which belonged to the Kingswood estate, while the other half was in the possession of Lord Marshwell, a neighbour with whom the Duke had little in common.

He thought that he would first ask at the farm if they had seen any sign of Benedicta, and if not, he would feel obliged to ride on to Lord Marshwell's land and perhaps find one of his farmers or keepers who might have noticed her.

He reached the farm, and to do so he had to ride round the corn-fields, and he noted as he did so that the sun had sunk and soon it would be dusk.

As he rode into the farm-yard a number of dogs came towards him, barking ferociously, and a voice with a broad Scots accent called:

"Wha' are ye blatherin' about, yon stupid beasties?"

The farmer came to the door and as the Duke dismounted he said:

"Why, it's yeerself, Yer Grace. I wasna expectin' ye to be visiting me at this hour o' the night!"

"I am not visiting you, McNab," the Duke replied, "except to enquire if you have seen a young lady walking through your fields."

"A young lady?" the farmer asked in astonishment. "And wha' would her be a-doing heere?"

"She left Kingswood early this afternoon," the Duke said, "and as she was moving north, I reckoned she would be somewhere in this vicinity."

"Weel, if that's so, I've had neither sight nor sound o' her," the old man said.

He looked across the yard and saw a milk-maid coming from the cow-shed with a pail of milk in her hands.

"Hi, Bessie," he called. "Have ye seen a young lady aboot the place today? His Grace be a-lookin' for her."

"A young lady?" Bessie repeated. "Nay, that Oi've not. But Oi were a-going to tell ye that a wee while ago Oi saw three men a-going into th' wood—poachers, like as not."

The farmer frowned.

"Poachers, I'd nay be surprised."

He looked at the Duke.

"Will ye tell yer keepers, Yer Grace, 'tis time they paid us a wee visit. There're poachers in th' woods right enough, and I've even heard shots in the last few weeks."

"I will tell them," the Duke replied. "And thank you for your information."

He mounted his horse, aware as he did so that the horse was tired and so was he.

"Gude-day to Yer Grace," the farmer said.

"Good-day, McNab," the Duke replied, then added: "I see your fields are looking in good shape."

"Aye, we should have a decent harvest, if Gawd be kind," the Scotsman replied.

The Duke rode out of the yard.

He would have liked to return home, but he knew that it would be impossible to until he was certain that Benedicta was not in the wood.

He did not like the idea of three rough men wandering about, and at the thought of them, every nerve in his body was suddenly tense with a fear such as he had never experienced for himself.

Supposing they found her, alone, perhaps asleep and unprotected? Supposing they assaulted her?

He felt that he wanted to cry out her name, to let her know that he was near and that he would fight for her and protect her.

But there was nothing he could do except ride on towards the wood.

When he reached it he saw that the undergrowth was thick and it would be difficult for a horse to move through it.

Dismounting, he tied the reins to a branch of a fallen tree, although he knew that in fact the animal would not wish to wander far.

Then, thinking that it was a hopeless task but one which he must undertake, he fought his way through the undergrowth and into the wood itself.

He soon found it easier to move amongst the tree-trunks to avoid the shrubs and brambles which caught at his clothes.

It was dark in the shadow of the branches and he thought apprehensively that it would be easy to lose his way.

Nevertheless, propelled by his anxiety for Benedicta and a fear for her that seemed to be growing every moment, he walked on, looking this way and that for any sign of a girl in a patched gown.

Then he heard voices.

He stood still to make quite sure that he was not mistaken, then he heard them again—men talking to each other.

He walked on and a few seconds later saw a light between the trunks of the trees.

The ground was covered with moss and there were patches of bluebells, which made it easy for him to move without being heard.

The Duke drew nearer and nearer to the light and now at last he could see a clearing where the wood-cutters had been working and in the centre of it was a small fire.

The three men were sitting round it.

One glance at them told the Duke that Bessie the milk-maid had not been mistaken when she had said they were rough-looking.

They were attired in ragged garments, which told the Duke that they were not countrymen but more likely had come from a town, perhaps London.

Each man carried, either beside him or across his knee, a stick with a heavy knobbled end, which the Duke knew could be a deadly weapon if used in combat on an opponent's head.

"I be footsore," one man complained in a grumbling tone when the Duke was within hearing.

"Us ain't got far t' go nah," another replied.

The last speaker was facing the Duke, who could see that he was a man of about twenty-five, dark-haired, with a brooding, surly look which was accentuated by a down-turned mouth.

He looked to be the kind of thug, the Duke thought, who would probably be a footpad or a criminal of some sort or other.

The other two men had their backs to him but he was sure that they were a similar type.

"'Ow much furver?" asked the man who had complained.

"I finks abaht eight mile," the other replied. "'Ave a rest 'ere an' we'll move on at dye-break."

"I be 'ungry, an' I 'ates th' country—it gives I the creeps!" the third man said.

This confirmed the Duke's impression that they were not countrymen.

The man facing him drew something from his pocket.

"P'raps this'll make ye feel better," he said. "Oi'll give ye th' money nah, case we 'as to separite after th' deed be done."

"I'm all f' that, Jeb," replied one of the men opposite him. "'Ow much do us get?"

"Wot Oi tells ye. Ten nah, an' there'll be twenty more when us gets back."

"Twenty!"

There was a note of awe in the voice of the man who had complained that he was hungry.

"Yus, twenty! An' on that us goes equal shares, but nah there's two 'jimmy o' goblins for ye an' four fer I."

"Four?"

"'Tis moi job, ain't it? Ye wouldn't be 'ere but fer I."

"Orl roight, but us shares th' next 'un."

"That's wot I says. Ye can believe I."

Jeb, who was facing the Duke, took the guineas out of a small bag and threw them one by one to the two men sitting on the other side of the fire.

They each caught a golden coin deftly, bit it with their teeth to see if it was real, then slipped it away into a pocket.

"S'posing when us gets there 'e don't come?" one of the men suggested

" 'E'll be there," Jeb replied. " 'E rides every morn' 'er says, an' 'e'll be alone."

" 'Ow does 'er know that?"

" 'Er knows!"

"An' s'posing 'e gallops orf?" one man suggested.

" 'E won't do that 'cause of what 'er tells we ter do. I told ye already, but ye don't listen."

"Tell us agin," the man said.

"Right, then. I lies 'alf under the pedge, scream-ing: *'Elp 'Elp!*"

"S'posing 'e tikes no notice?"

" 'E'll tike notice orl roight, 'cause 'e'll think as 'ow me legs've caught in a gin-trap."

"Wot 'appens then?"

" 'E gets orf 'is 'orse an' comes to 'elp I, an' as 'e bends over I, ye slug 'im 'ard on the head! Knock 'im down, an' if 'e ain't dead, then I'll finish 'im orf!"

"That be murder, Jeb!" one of the men said gloomily.

"Wot o' it?" enquired the man who had given them the guineas. "Ye've been paid, ain't ye? But, Charlie, tell I th' truth. D'ye wanter go back? If ye does, ye can give I back 'em guineas!"

"Na, it's orl roight," Charlie replied. "But ye're certain 'e'll be alone?"

"If there's anyone wiv 'im, we'll deal wiv 'em, we'll see 'em coming, an' it'll give us time ter pull a kerchief over our faces."

"Looks loik ye've thought o' everythin'," Charlie remarked.

"I 'ave!" Jeb said complacently. "An' all we've

got do when it's over is skip back t' London an' tell 'er Lidyship to 'and over the dibs."

"And supposing she does nothing of the sort?" a voice questioned.

If the men round the fire were startled, so was the Duke, for stepping from behind Jeb into the light of the fire came Benedicta!

She had nothing on her head and she was wearing the darned, patched gown with the little white collar in which he had seen her first.

She seemed, the Duke thought, to be enveloped in a strange light, but she was alone—alone with these men, who, he realised, had been sent to kill him.

He wondered frantically what he should do.

He was not afraid for his own safety, but there were three of them, and while they carried their knotted sticks, which he knew could kill a man with one well-directed blow, he had nothing in his hands except his thin riding-whip.

For a moment he was indecisive, then he heard Benedicta say:

"It is Jeb Cutler, is it not?"

"'Ow did ye know?" Jeb exclaimed truculently, then added, "Why, 'tis Miss Benedicta!"

"Yes, Benedicta Calvine, and I see that you have not forgotten me or my father."

"Now, Miss Benedicta, 'ow be th' Reverend?"

"He is dead, Jeb. And how do you think he feels when he knows that after all he did for you, after all you promised, you are planning a crime so terrible, so wicked, that I cannot bear to think of it."

Jeb fidgeted uncomfortably.

"Well, 'tis loik this, Miss Benedicta—th' lidy sends for I, an' she offers I so much 'twas 'ard to refuse."

"Money to kill a man? Oh, Jeb, you promised, you promised that you would go straight if Papa could persuade the Governor to reduce your sentence."

"I were grateful, Miss Benedicta. I were reelly!" Jeb said. "But times be 'ard, an' me old Ma don't get enough t' eat."

"She would have enough if you worked for it, Jeb," Benedicta said quietly.

" 'Ere! Wot's a-goin' on?" Charlie asked from the other side of the fire. "Who's this 'ere goil?"

"Ye speak to 'er polite-like," Jeb said fiercely. "This 'ere young lidy's father got I out o' prison 'cause 'e believed I were innocent—which I were. 'E speaks t' th' Guv'nor, an' he sets I free."

"I asked you a question," Benedicta said. "What do you think my father feels now?"

"Ye said 'e were dead."

"And so he is, Jeb. But you know that he believed, as I do, that when one dies one only goes to another world, where one can still help those we loved when we were on earth. Papa will still be wanting to help you, but how can he do so if you commit this wicked act?"

There was a silence, then one of the men said:

"Ye don't know, Miss, wot it's loik to go 'ungry an' yer children a-cryin' fer somethin' t' eat."

"They will be hungrier still if you are caught and hanged for this crime," Benedicta answered.

"Jeb says as 'ow us won't be caught."

"Do you really imagine that if you kill a nobleman of such importance as the Duke of Kingswood you will get away with it?" Benedicta asked.

There was silence before she continued:

"Within hours the whole country will be alive with troops searching for you, and there will be no time for you to get back to London. Your children will cry for their father, and Jeb's mother for her son, and what good will your gold be then?"

She paused for a moment to let what she had said sink in, then she said:

"I know the lady who has bribed you to carry out this dastardly deed on her behalf, and even if you are not found and arrested before you reach London, I very much doubt if she will pay you what she has promised."

" 'Er'd better—or else!" Jeb said furiously.

"And how can you make her?" Benedicta asked. "Supposing when you go back and tell her that the murder has been done, she hands you over to the Bow Street Runners? They will also be looking for you, and there are few places in London where you can hide from them."

"Oi tells ye—Oi tells ye Oi didn't loik th' sound o' it!" Charlie wailed in a nervous voice. "Oi don't loik th' country—'tis too quiet!"

Benedicta looked down at Jeb, and the Duke, watching her, thought that in the light from the fire there was a spiritual expression on her face which made her look as if she had stepped from one of the paintings of saints which hung on the walls at Kingswood.

"I am sorry, Jeb, that your mother is ill," she said quietly, "and I know you love her, but I think it would kill her if she knew you were to be hanged."

"Stop it, Miss Benedicta!" Jeb cried. "Loik Charlie says, ye're a-givin' I th' creeps!"

"I think that what I am doing," Benedicta contradicted, "is awakening your conscience. I think too, Jeb, that you are afraid to offend Papa, who helped you so much. Can you imagine how humiliated he would be to know that he trusted someone who was not worthy of that trust, and believed in a man who was not truthful, and not innocent."

"I were innocent o' that job, Miss," Jeb interrupted. "I did tell the Reverend th' truth."

"Then do not spoil everything now," Benedicta begged.

Suddenly she raised her voice to say:

"You are being very foolish not only to risk being hanged for the ghastly crime of murder, but also, because you do not understand country ways, to linger here with a lighted fire in the centre of a wood. If the game-keepers catch you, you will be charged with poaching, and you should be aware that the penalty for that is transportation—banishment to a penal-colony."

The three men rose to their feet.

"Oi always said as Oi didn't loik th' country," Charlie grumbled.

"Go back to London," Benedicta said firmly. "Keep the money you already have, but do not go near that lady who gave it to you. But you must not keep one penny of this blood-money for yourselves. You, Jeb, must spend it on your mother; and you others, on your children or your wives. But not on yourselves personally. Is that understood?"

"Yus, Miss," Jeb murmured, while the other two men made inarticulate sounds.

"Then go, and hurry," Benedicta said. "While you are here you are trespassing, and it would be foolish to be convicted for such a minor crime when I have saved you from committing a far more serious one."

The two men on the other side of the fire turned away, but as Jeb would have followed them Benedicta laid her hand on his arm.

"I shall be praying for you, Jeb," she said. "Praying that my father was not mistaken and that at heart you are, as he believed you to be, a good man."

"It's 'ard, Miss Benedicta," Jeb muttered.

"I know," she said, "but when you are tempted again, remember that both my father and I will be praying for you, praying very hard, Jeb."

Jeb did not reply, but merely pulled his torn cap farther over his eyes and slouched away, following the other two men through the trees on a path made by the wood-cutters.

Benedicta stood watching them until finally Jeb was out of sight, then she sat down and covered her face with her hands.

It was only then that the Duke moved.

He could hardly believe what he had seen and heard.

Yet he knew that there had been no need for him to interfere because Benedicta had handled everything in such an amazing way.

As he had watched her, he had felt certain that

she was surrounded by a kind of celestial light which he had perceived when she first appeared.

It might have been part of the shimmering of the fire where the men had sat listening to her, but he was convinced that it was something different, something which shone from within herself.

He approached her quietly, and only when he was actually standing beside her did she look up questioningly, as if she thought perhaps Jeb had returned with something further to say to her.

When she saw who stood there, she gave a little cry which seemed to come from her very heart.

"I have come to take you home, Benedicta," the Duke said gently.

Chapter Seven

Benedicta sprang to her feet and by the light of the fire the Duke could see that she was very pale, and yet there was a sudden radiance in her eyes which he had seen before, when he had returned home from London.

"You are ... here!" she said at length, wonderingly.

"Yes, I am here," he replied, "and I heard you save my life."

She gave a little shudder as if the horror of it was still with her. Then she looked towards the darkness of the trees where the men had disappeared and said:

"You must be ... careful. I am sure that now they will not do what they ... intended to do, but I cannot trust them ... completely."

"You saved me," the Duke repeated, "and now you must look after me. I will take you home, Benedicta."

She looked at him as if for a moment what he had said did not penetrate her mind. Then she replied in a low voice:

"I ... cannot come with ... you."

"Why not?"

"Because I have to ... go away ... I cannot ... do what you ... ask."

"I realise that now," he answered, "and I have something different to suggest to you."

145

He moved a step nearer, but she put up her hands as if to ward him off.

"N-no," she said, "I must . . . go. . . . I am going to my . . . grandfather in . . . Northumberland. I think he will . . . forgive me . . . and take me in."

"You intend walking all that way by yourself?" the Duke asked.

"I shall be . . . all right."

"I doubt it," he replied. "And if you wish to go to Northumberland I will take you there, but I would rather you come home first. It is growing dark, Benedicta, and we cannot stay here talking all night."

Again she looked towards the path down which the men had gone. Then as if she was frightened she put out her hands towards him.

"Go away," she said. "I am afraid . . . afraid for you."

"As I have been for you," the Duke replied. "I cannot tell you, Benedicta, what agonies I have been through since I started searching for you early this afternoon."

She looked at him with an expression which he thought was one of surprise, and he added:

"Did you really think I would let you leave me?"

"I have . . . to go," she repeated. "I want to obey you . . . but I cannot . . . marry Richard."

"You are not going to marry Richard," the Duke said softly. "You are going to marry me, Benedicta—if you will have me."

He saw that she did not understand, and she looked at him with a puzzled expression in her eyes. Then as her eyes met his she grew very still.

"Wh-what are you . . . saying?" she asked.

The words were so low that they were little more than a whisper.

"I am telling you, my darling," the Duke said, "that I cannot live without you. It is a long story, which I will tell you as we ride home, but now I am asking you to return to Kingswood and take care of me, as you did just now when those men were plotting to kill me."

For a long moment Benedicta just looked at him.

Then he saw her face transformed by a radiance which made her so beautiful that it seemed once again as if she was enveloped with a celestial light.

"Do you mean ... do you really ... mean ..." she stammered.

The Duke put his arms round her.

"I mean that I love you!" he said. "As I have loved you for a very long time, but I would not acknowledge it to myself."

She made a little sound that was indescribable, then hid her face against his shoulder.

"I love you!" the Duke repeated. "And I think, my precious one, that you already love me a little."

"I love you!" she whispered. "But I never dreamt ... I never thought ..."

"I know," he answered, "but what I feel for you can no longer be denied. Let us go home."

As she raised her head to look up at him, his lips captured hers.

He held her fiercely against him, and yet his lips were gentle, and he kissed her in a way that he had never kissed another woman, because there was something reverent in his feelings for her.

To Benedicta, the Duke's kiss was a wonder and a glory beyond anything which she had ever imagined or of which she had ever dreamt.

She had never before been kissed, but she had always believed that a kiss between two people in love was part of the Divine Blessing from God.

Now she felt as if she had stepped from the mundane world into Heaven, and as the Duke's lips became more insistent, more possessive, she thought that perhaps she had died and was no longer human.

He held her closer still, and now she knew that behind the tenderness there was a fire which she sensed rather than understood.

When at length the Duke raised his head, he looked down into her eyes, which were filled with light, and saw the softness of her parted lips, and he knew that he had found what all men seek.

"I love you!" he said, and because the words were new to him they sounded strange even to his own ears.

He put his arm round her and drew her back along the path by which he had come.

It was hard to walk together but by being so close, as if they were one person, they managed it; and finally, struggling through the undergrowth on the outside of the wood, they came to where the Duke had left his horse.

It was now nearly dusk, and yet it seemed to the Duke as if the sunlight was still in Benedicta's eyes.

"It is a long way home, my beloved," he said. "Shall we go to the farm and see if we can borrow a pony and trap, or shall we go slowly on my horse?"

"It will perhaps be ... uncomfortable for you."

The Duke smiled.

"The only alternative is to walk," he said, "and I think you have done enough of that for one day."

Benedicta gave a little laugh.

"I confess I have not travelled as far as I had hoped," she said, "but the truth is that the shoes which Mrs. Newall gave me were a little too small and I could not move as quickly as I would have wished."

"I am grateful for that," the Duke said, "for I might have had to look farther for you, and I might not have heard those men in the wood planning my murder."

"I could not ... believe that ... anyone could be so ... wicked," Benedicta said with a little throb in her voice.

The Duke knew that she was speaking of Delyth Maulden.

"Forget her," he said.

He had reached his horse, and now he pulled off his riding-coat and laid it on the front of his saddle. Then he picked Benedicta up in his arms and set her on it before he mounted behind her.

As he put his right arm round her and held the reins with his left, he asked:

"You are comfortable?"

She was shy because she was close against him and she could feel his heart, beneath his thin lawn shirt, beating against her breast.

"Very ... comfortable," she answered in a very little voice, and the Duke smiled because he knew that she was blushing.

He pulled her even closer against him and kissed her lips before he spurred his horse forward.

They travelled slowly, and the Duke thought that however long it took, he could imagine no journey that could be so entrancing as to have Benedicta in his arms.

"When did you first know you loved me?" he asked as they circled the growing corn in the valley.

"I think I loved you the first ... moment I saw you," Benedicta replied. "You were ... so kind about Papa ... and then when I saw you sitting in your high-backed chair in the Dining-Room, I thought no man could be so magnificent ... or look so important."

She gave a little sigh.

"I felt sadly out-of-place in my rags and tatters ... but you talked to me as if you were interested in what I said, and ... no-one else could have been such a ... great gentleman."

The Duke kissed her hair before he said:

"Major Haverington warned me that you might fall in love with me, but you hid it very successfully."

"And yet ... you knew I ... loved you?"

"Richard told me so."

"Richard?"

"When I found that you had gone, I went to his room and asked him if he knew where you had gone. He told me he thought you would have gone back to the North. He also said he did not wish to marry you, because you loved me."

"You must have ... thought it very ... impertinent of me," Benedicta murmured.

The Duke gave a little laugh.

"I thought it was not only the most wonderful thing I had ever heard but also, although I would not acknowledge it, what I had longed for."

"I thought you . . . wished never to marry."

"I swore I would never do so," the Duke agreed, "but that was before I met you."

"Did I . . . really make you . . . change your mind?"

"You are the first and only woman I have ever asked to marry me," the Duke said, "and the only one I have ever wanted as my wife!"

"How . . . can you . . . want me?" Benedicta asked. "I have . . . nothing to offer you, except . . . my love."

"Which to me is the most priceless thing in the world," the Duke replied; "so priceless, my precious one, that I value it far more than Kingswood or anything else I possess."

Benedicta looked up at him.

"Do you . . . really mean that?"

"I will convince you that it is the truth."

Then as if he could not help himself he drew his horse to a standstill and kissed her until she could only cling to him, breathless and enchanted.

Her heart was beating against his and the flame she had sensed behind his lips was also a part of her.

* * *

It took them a long time to reach Kingswood and when at last they could see it silhouetted against the sky, the lights in the windows glowing golden in the darkness, Benedicta said:

"It is so big and impressive, and you are of such . . . consequence . . . you should not marry a nobody . . . like me. I ought to . . . refuse you."

"And do you think I would let you?" the Duke asked.

"How can I . . . be a Duchess?" Benedicta asked, with a sudden frightened note in her voice as if she had just thought of it. "I shall . . . make mistakes . . . I shall do the wrong things, and perhaps you will ... regret that you ever brought me ... back."

"That is so unlikely that I cannot even consider the possibility," the Duke said with a smile. "All I know is, however ignorant you may be of the Social World, my darling one, you have something which will always tell you what is right and what is wrong."

"What is that?" Benedicta enquired.

"I think most people would call it instinct," the Duke answered, "but I believe it is something which comes from the soul, and that it was that which I saw shining round you like a light when you were talking to those thugs."

"Did you really ... see that?" she asked in a low voice.

"I promise you that when you came from behind the tree to speak to them, there seemed to be a light about you—a light that came from within."

"I wish I could believe that was true," Benedicta said. "It is what Papa told me came from those who are inspired: the Prophets, the Disciples, and other great Leaders of men."

She gave a little sigh that was one of happiness and put her head back against his shoulder.

"I thought perhaps you would have the same light about you ... when you went into battle ... knowing you were fighting a just cause.... If I had it then in the wood, it was because I was fighting for you."

"That is the sensible explanation, my lovely one," the Duke said, "but I think that it is in fact the light of purity from someone who is good in a world filled with wickedness and evil."

"No ... no, that is not true!" Benedicta protested. "You only think that, because Jeb was tempted into trying to ... kill you for money. Papa said there is good in everybody, and there is good in Jeb too. He is kind to his mother, and when I awakened his conscience he went away."

The Duke's lips lingered for a moment on her forehead, then he said:

"You are arguing with me again, and I think, my darling, that we shall always enjoy our arguments; but I shall still stick to my own conviction that there is a Power greater than ourselves, who sent you to save me. That is what you have done, and now I am your responsibility for the rest of your life."

"I can imagine nothing more ... wonderful," Benedicta whispered.

"You have saved not only me," the Duke said as they rounded the lake and rode towards the bridge.

"Who else have I saved?" Benedicta asked.

"Richard," the Duke replied, "because once we are married, which I intend will happen as soon as possible, Delyth Maulden will no longer wish to marry him. So he is free. He shall go to India as soon as he is well enough."

"Oh, I am glad ... so very ... very glad!" Benedicta cried.

* * *

The Duke rose from the dining-table, where they had been sitting for a long time, and drew Benedicta to her feet.

They had found so much to talk about that they had lingered on long after the servants had left them alone.

The table was decorated with white gardenias and there were the same flowers arranged in Benedicta's hair. They were also in the bouquet she had carried when a few hours earlier she had married the Duke in the private Chapel where her father had lain in state before his burial.

It had been a very quiet, almost secret Service, with just the senior servants present, and of course Richard, who had insisted that he should be carried downstairs in a chair so that he could attend the wedding.

"If I were well enough I would take you up the aisle on my arm," he had said to Benedicta, "but as it is, I am going to be there to see that Cousin Nolan really and truly renounces his bachelorhood for the bonds of matrimony."

He laughed.

"I still cannot believe that after all he said and all the women who have tried to capture him, it should be you who is leading him to the altar."

"I have told him that I am the ... wrong wife for him," Benedicta said humbly.

"Nonsense! You are the right one, exactly right," Richard corrected.

He spoke so positively that Benedicta looked at him in surprise.

"Why do you say that?"

"Because—do you not see?—you are different from all the other women," Richard replied. "They loved him, but they all believed that his heart was locked away in a barred prison, or else was nonexistent."

"I still cannot ... believe that I have found it!" Benedicta said almost beneath her breath.

"But you have," Richard assured her, "and I have never known Cousin Nolan to look so happy or to be so kind and understanding."

"I am so lucky ... so tremendously ... unbelievably lucky."

"And so is he," Richard said. "You are just the sort of wife he should have."

"I cannot think why you should say that."

"Well, for one thing, because you stand up to him," Richard answered, "another, because you are clever. Cousin Nolan has a brilliant brain and he soon becomes bored with those cork-brained creatures who simper at him all the time. They never lasted more than six months."

"You are making me nervous!" Benedicta cried. "Supposing after six months he is sorry he ever married me?"

Richard smiled.

"In which case I will come back from India and run away with you," he said. "I have a feeling that in the future I am going to regret not having married you myself when I had the chance."

"You will fall in love one day," Benedicta said, "and then it will be with the right person, and everything will be perfect as it is with the Duke and me."

She looked so happy as she spoke and love had made her so beautiful that Richard found himself staring at her as if he had never really seen her before.

And that was how the Duke felt when he saw her in her wedding-gown, with a tiara from the Kingswood collection holding her veil in place.

He had gone to her bed-room to collect her for the wedding-ceremony. It had not been the room she had occupied on the second floor, but the State Bed-room where the Duchesses of Kingswood had always slept and which communicated with his.

When he had knocked on the door, it was Mrs. Newall who had called, "Come in!" before Benedicta could reply.

Then, as if she sensed who was there, she turned from the dressing-table to stand looking at him.

Because her veil did not yet cover her face he could see her eyes clearly, and he thought that no woman could look more lovely or more loving.

"Nolan!"

He thought that the way she spoke his name seemed to express everything that was within her heart.

"Your Grace!" Mrs. Newall said, then she curtseyed and withdrew from the room to hurry down the stairs to take her place in the Chapel.

"I have come to fetch you, my darling," the Duke said. "Everyone is ready, including the Vicar, and I for one cannot wait any longer."

Benedicta moved towards him and he thought she looked like a nymph who had risen from the mist which covered the lake in the early morning.

There was something ethereal about her. But she no longer looked like the lost waif as she had done when he had seen her across her father's grave and longed to comfort and protect her.

Now she had an assurance and a new confidence, which he knew came because he had given her his loving and because her feelings for him were so overwhelming that she found it hard to express them.

As she reached his side, she looked up at him and said:

"You are sure ... quite sure that even at this last moment you ... would not wish to remain a bachelor? If you have ... changed your mind ... I will ... understand."

"And if I did, what would you feel?" the Duke asked.

Benedicta drew in her breath.

"It would ... break my heart to lose you," she said, "but you know that above everything else I want your happiness ... and that is why I want you to feel ... free, if that is ... what you wish."

The Duke put his fingers under her chin and tipped her face up to his.

"I can never be free again," he said. "I am caught, captured, and completely conquered, my darling, by an enemy against which there is no defence."

"An ... enemy?"

"That is what I believed love to be," the Duke answered, "but now I know I was wrong, and if you think you can lose me you are very much mistaken. Come! I am more impatient than I can possibly say to make you my wife."

As he finished speaking, his lips were on hers and she knew without further words that what he had said was true.

He wanted her, desired her, and yet there was something so much deeper in their relationship that she knew he was right when he said he was conquered.

He was hers and she was his, and there was no possible escape for either of them.

Very gently the Duke drew the veil over Benedicta's face; then, with her arm through his and his other hand covering hers, they walked down the Grand Staircase side by side.

The Chapel was a bower of flowers, and the dozen servants sitting at the back, and Richard, who was in the front pew, were so unobtrusive as to make Benedicta feel as if she and the Duke were alone in the presence of God.

Every word of the Service seemed to beat in her mind like the music of angels, and she felt that both her father and mother were near her and were over-whelmingly glad that she had found love as they had.

After the ceremony, they had cut the cake, which had been made by the Chef, and had been toasted in champagne until the Duke had said firmly that Richard must go to bed, because he was looking tired.

Then at last they were alone, but only for a short while before it was time for dinner, and they walked into the great Dining-Room to sit in a little oasis of light at the flower-decked table.

It made Benedicta feel that it could not be only four days ago that the Duke had said:

"When Richard is better and your trousseau is ready I will take you abroad, but because I want to marry you as quickly as possible, I am only going to wait until one gown is ready—the one you will wear at your wedding."

Because Benedicta was so happy for him to plan everything for her, she had agreed, and she had not really been surprised when the gown arrived within three days and with it a multitude of exquisitely made but more intimate garments, which the Duke had ordered from London.

No-one, he had decided, should know about the wedding until it had actually taken place, and there was every excuse for secrecy as Benedicta was in mourning.

There was also a need for speed, and Benedicta approved of this because as the Duke had said, once it was known that they were married, Delyth Maulden would no longer pursue Richard.

She was in fact terrified that, having failed in her first attempt to murder the Duke, Lady Delyth would try something else.

Every time the Duke left the house she was afraid, and she insisted on riding with him every morning.

Although she had never expressed her fears for him, he was well aware that she looked round her apprehensively every time they were in a wood or near a thick hedge from which some assailant might appear.

Tonight, when dinner was over and they walked back along the corridor to the Salon, Benedicta said:

"I keep feeling I am in a dream . . . but as long as I can hold on to you . . . as long as you are beside me . . . I shall gradually become convinced that what is happening is . . . real."

"I will convince you, my precious," the Duke answered.

They walked into the Salon and Benedicta saw that all the curtains were drawn with the exception of those covering a long French window which opened onto the terrace.

She went towards it and the Duke said:

"I thought that tonight of all nights we ought to look at the stars and think how lucky we are that out of the millions of planets in the universe, we have found each other."

"So very . . . very lucky," Benedicta said. "At the same time . . . I think it is all . . . planned that we should . . . meet and we should . . . love each other."

"I do not mind how it happened," the Duke answered, "but it has, and that is what is important."

He put his arm round her and drew her through the window and onto the terrace.

It was a warm night, with no wind, and a mist rose above the lake and swirled round the trunks of the trees in the Park.

The stars were brilliant in the sky and there was a crescent moon climbing amongst them.

Benedicta threw back her head to look up.

"Could anything be more beautiful or inspiring?"

"That is what I thought when I saw you."

She smiled shyly at him, then turned so as to be close in his arms.

"I love you! I love you!" she cried. "I cannot think of anything else and there seem to be no other words in which to tell you how I feel."

"That is what I want to say to you," the Duke said, "not once but a thousand times; and now, my darling, there is nothing to stop me from saying it, because you are mine."

She lifted her face for him to kiss her, but to her surprise he was looking not at her but still up at the sky. Then he said:

"Before you came into my life I questioned many things: whether there was a God, whether there was any plan in the universe, and certainly whether there was any survival after death."

Benedicta listened, for she had never heard him speak so seriously.

"Then, my darling," he continued, "I found you, and you have given me not only an indescribable happiness and a love I had never thought to find, but also quite a new conception of everything we are and everything mankind strives to become."

"Have I . . . really done that?"

"You have, but there is so much more I want to learn, and that is what you have to teach me."

"Tell me . . . what you want," Benedicta murmured.

"I think everybody yearns for faith," the Duke said, "and because that is what you have, it shines from you like a light from the stars above. That is what I want you to give me, as well as the inestimable gift of yourself."

"It is what I want to give you, my darling husband," Benedicta replied. "It is something which we must give to our children, so that they never doubt that God is there to help and protect them."

"Our children..." the Duke said quietly, almost beneath his breath.

Benedicta lifted her arms and put them round his neck.

"I know what Kingswood means to you and your family," she whispered. "That is why I must, my precious husband, not only love you with all my heart and soul, but also, if God is willing, give you an heir who can carry on the traditions of your great family."

The Duke drew in his breath.

He knew that this was what he wanted, what had been in the back of his mind, and he thought no-one but Benedicta would have spoken so frankly or so sweetly.

"You know that is what I want," he said in his deep voice, "and I can imagine nothing more perfect than that we should have children born of our love."

"That is what I am...trying to say," Benedicta said, "and...oh, Nolan, I love you so desperately, and I feel that only by giving you a son who is as wonderful as you will I be able to express how much you mean to me."

The Duke's arms went round her and he kissed her fiercely and with a passion which she had not known from him before.

And yet she knew there was still something other-worldly between them, something that seemed part of the stars, the mist, and the vows they had made in the Chapel.

The Duke kissed her for a long time, then at last he said:

"Let us go upstairs, my darling one. I want to be closer to you than I can be at this moment. I want to make you mine so that never again will we be two separate people, but one."

He drew her into the Salon, and then, quietly and without speaking, they walked up the stairs towards the historic rooms where so many Duchesses had lived, loved, and contributed to the history not only of the family but of England.

When they entered Benedicta's bed-room the candles were alight and there was a small fire in the grate, but there was nobody waiting for her.

She looked a little questioningly at the Duke, and he said:

"I ordered that nobody was to wait up for us tonight, neither a maid for you nor Hawkins for me. We would just be alone."

"That is ... exactly what I would ... like," Benedicta said, "and yet ... I feel a little ... shy, because I shall have to ... ask you to ... undo my ... g-gown."

She saw the smile on his lips and she added:

"I feel sure you are very ... experienced at doing ... such things."

"Does that make you jealous?" the Duke asked. "I assure you, my darling, you need not be jealous of the past, for I have never, and this is the truth, felt as I feel now."

"What ... do you feel?"

"Younger than my years, happier than I have ever been in my whole life, and very, very much in love."

Benedicta gave a little cry and threw herself against him.

"Go on feeling like that," she begged. "Oh, darling, I am so frightened that I may ... disappoint you."

She hid her face against his shoulder and said in a voice he could hardly hear:

"Richard said that I was the right wife for you because I was so intelligent ... but at this moment I am very ... ignorant ... and I know so little ... that I may ... disappoint you."

The Duke's eyes were very tender as he pulled her closer to him.

"Do you think I want you to know anything but what I shall teach you?" he asked. "I adore your ignorance, I love you when you are shy, and most of

all I worship you because you are pure and untouched."

There was something in the way he spoke which
made Benedicta know that he was telling her something which moved him deeply.

"I knew without your telling me that I was the
first man who had ever kissed you," the Duke said,
"and I shall be the first man to touch your exquisite
body and to possess you. I shall also be the only man,
and the last."

He spoke fiercely and with a note in his voice
that was almost menacing.

Benedicta looked up at him and saw a sudden
hardness in his eyes and a sharpness to the lines of
his mouth, which surprised her.

"How could there be anybody else but you?" she
asked. "You know that I would not marry Richard because I did not love him. Do you imagine that I
could ever find another man who could interest me?"

She moved a little closer as she said:

"In the whole world there is only you . . . and you
. . . and you . . . and I love you with . . . all of me."

Her words seemed to vibrate between them, and
now he looked down at her, seeing her eyes, wide
and very young and with a touch of bewilderment in
them because she did not understand why he was
speaking as he was.

He knew that her innocence and purity was all
he ever wanted, all he had ever thought to find in a
woman he could make his wife.

He knew too that in the love that would make
them one, all that had hurt and wounded him in the
past would be swept away.

The barriers he had created round himself because of what he had discovered about his mother
had fallen.

The shrine in his heart which she had spoilt and
defamed was no longer empty. Benedicta was there,
filling it completely, surrounding it with the light
which came from her soul and which was the celestial
light of the Divine.

He looked down at her, sensing with a new perception the little fear that he had evoked by the harshness of his words.

She was uncertain, unsure not of her love but of his, and he knew at that moment that the past was swept away as if by a great tidal-wave, and the future glowed golden ahead.

There was only the present—the present, when he had come into his Kingdom and found that the impossible was possible.

The last battle had been fought, the last enemy of doubt defeated.

Very tenderly he looked down into Benedicta's eyes.

He knew that later tonight they would be able to talk more freely; he could tell her what was in his heart, and express his thankfulness for the wonder and glory of their love.

But now, at the moment, there was no need for words but those that came spontaneously in the rapture of knowing that she was his.

His lips came down on hers and his arms crushed her against him.

"You are mine!" he said. "Mine, my precious darling, and I will love you from now until eternity, as you will love me."

He kissed her until he felt her soft and pliant against him and knew that his lips had awakened in her the first flickering flames of desire.

It was then that gently he undid the buttons at the back of her gown.

He felt her tremble for a moment, but it was not only with shyness, but because of the new sensations he was arousing within her, which she had never felt before.

He kissed her eyes, her cheeks, her lips, and the little pulse that was beating in her throat.

Then as her gown slipped to the floor he lifted her in his arms.

"This is how I carried you once before," he said,

"and I knew then that you were mine and I could never lose you."

"I ... love you ... Nolan!" Benedicta whispered. "I love you ... and you make me feel very ... strange and ... very excited."

"That is what I want you to feel," the Duke said.

He laid her down on the great silk-canopied bed, blew out the candles, and a moment later was beside her, holding her in his arms.

He felt a tremor run through her, and he too was excited and aroused as he had never been before in any of his love-affairs.

This was different—this was a woman whom he not only desired with his body but also with his mind, his heart, and his soul.

He brushed Benedicta's hair back from her forehead so that he could look at her face and he thought no-one could look so beautiful.

It was not only the perfection of her features but something spiritual in her expression, and her eyes, which drew him as if there were a shaft of starlight drawing him up into the sky.

He bent his head to find her lips, and when his hand touched her body he felt them tremble together.

Then there was only the ecstasy, rapture, and glory of God, which a man and woman, joined as one, find when their love is pure and innocent of evil.

ABOUT THE AUTHOR

BARBARA CARTLAND, the world's most famous romantic novelist, who is also an historian, playwright, lecturer, political speaker and television personality, has now written over 200 books. She has also had many historical works published and has written four autobiographies as well as the biographies of her mother and that of her brother Ronald Cartland, who was the first Member of Parliament to be killed in the last war. This book has a preface by Sir Winston Churchill. Barbara Cartland has sold 80 million books over the world, more than half of these in the U.S.A. She broke the world record in 1975 by writing twenty books, and her own record in 1976 with twenty-one. In private life, Barbara Cartland, who is a Dame of the Order of St. John of Jerusalem, has fought for better conditions and salaries for Midwives and Nurses. As President of the Royal College of Midwives (Hertfordshire Branch), she has been invested with the first Badge of Office ever given in Great Britain, which was subscribed to by the Midwives themselves. She has also championed-the-cause for old people and founded the first Romany Gypsy Camp in the world. Barbara Cartland is deeply interested in Vitamin Therapy and is President of the British National Association for Health.

BARBARA CARTLAND
PRESENTS
THE ANCIENT WISDOM SERIES

The world's all-time bestselling author of romantic fiction, Barbara Cartland, has established herself as High Priestess of Love in its purest and most traditionally romantic form.

"We have," she says, "in the last few years thrown out the spiritual aspect of love and concentrated only on the crudest and most debased sexual side.

"Love at its highest has inspired mankind since the beginning of time. Civilization's greatest pictures, music, prose and poetry have all been written under the influence of love. This love is what we all seek despite the temptations of the sensuous, the erotic, the violent and the perversions of pornography.

"I believe that for the young and the idealistic, my novels with their pure heroines and high ideals are a guide to happiness. Only by seeking the Divine Spark which exists in every human being, can we create a future built on the foundation of faith."

Barbara Cartland is also well known for her Library of Love, classic tales of romance, written by famous authors like Elinor Glyn and Ethel M. Dell, which have been personally selected and specially adapted for today's readers by Miss Cartland.

"These novels I have selected and edited for my 'Library of Love' are all stories with which the readers can identify themselves and also be assured that right will triumph in the end. These tales elevate and activate the mind rather than debase it as so many modern stories do."

Now, in August, Bantam presents the first four novels in a new Barbara Cartland Ancient Wisdom series. The books are THE FORBIDDEN CITY by Barbara Cartland, herself; THE ROMANCE OF TWO WORLDS by Marie Corelli; THE HOUSE OF FULFILLMENT by L. Adams Beck; and BLACK LIGHT by Talbot Mundy.

"Now I am introducing something which I think is of vital importance at this moment in history. Following my own autobiographical book I SEEK THE MIRACULOUS, which Dutton is publishing in hardcover this summer, I am offering those who seek 'the world behind the world' novels which contain, besides a fascinating story, the teaching of Ancient Wisdom.

"In the snow-covered vastnesses of the Himalayas, there are lamaseries filled with manuscripts which have been kept secret for century upon century. In the depths of the tropical jungles and the arid wastes of the deserts, there are also those who know the esoteric mysteries which few can understand.

"Yet some of their precious and sacred knowledge has been revealed to writers in the past. These books I have collected, edited and offer them to those who want to look beyond this greedy, grasping, materialistic world to find their own souls.

"I believe that Love, human and divine, is the jail-breaker of that prison of selfhood which confines and confuses us . . .

"I believe that for those who have attained enlightenment, super-normal (not super-human) powers are available to those who seek them."

All Barbara Cartland's own novels and her Library of Love are available in Bantam Books, wherever paperbacks are sold. Look for her Ancient Wisdom Series to be available in August.

Barbara Cartland

The world's bestselling author of romantic fiction. Her stories are always captivating tales of intrigue, adventure and love.

☐	11372	LOVE AND THE LOATHSOME LEOPARD	$1.50
☐	11410	THE NAKED BATTLE	$1.50
☐	11512	THE HELL-CAT AND THE KING	$1.50
☐	11537	NO ESCAPE FROM LOVE	$1.50
☐	11580	THE CASTLE MADE FOR LOVE	$1.50
☐	11579	THE SIGN OF LOVE	$1.50
☐	11595	THE SAINT AND THE SINNER	$1.50
☐	11649	A FUGITIVE FROM LOVE	$1.50
☐	11797	THE TWISTS AND TURNS OF LOVE	$1.50
☐	11801	THE PROBLEMS OF LOVE	$1.50
☐	11751	LOVE LEAVES AT MIDNIGHT	$1.50
☐	11882	MAGIC OR MIRAGE	$1.50
☐	10712	LOVE LOCKED IN	$1.50
☐	11959	LORD RAVENSCAR'S REVENGE	$1.50
☐	11488	THE WILD, UNWILLING WIFE	$1.50
☐	11555	LOVE, LORDS, AND LADY-BIRDS	$1.50